REALLY UNUSUAL
BAD BOYS

REALLY UNUSUAL
BAD BOYS

MARYJANICE DAVIDSON

BRAVA

KENSINGTON PUBLISHING CORP.
http://www.kensingtonbooks.com

BRAVA BOOKS are published by

Kensington Publishing Corp.
850 Third Avenue
New York, NY 10022

All Kensington titles, imprints and distributed lines are available at special quantity discounts for bulk purchases for sales promotion, premiums, fund-raising, educational or institutional use.

Special book excerpts or customized printings can also be created to fit specific needs. For details, write or phone the office of the Kensington Special Sales Manager: Kensington Publishing Corp., 850 Third Avenue, New York, NY 10022. Attn. Special Sales Department. Phone: 1-800-221-2647.

ISBN 0-7582-0891-X

First Kensington Trade Paperback Printing: September 2005
10   9   8   7   6   5   4   3   2

Printed in the United States of America

For the fans of Canis Royal,
who wanted to know how it ended.

ACKNOWLEDGMENTS

Many thanks to Officer Lynn Ristau of the Superior Police Department, for patiently answering all my questions, and Jessica L. Growette, the greatest pharmacist in the world. Her bosses should worship her. Any mistakes you see are mine, not theirs.

Oh that the desert were my dwelling place,
With one fair spirit for my minister,
That I might all forget the human race,
And hating no one, love but only her!
—Lord Byron, *Childe Harold's Pilgrimage*

A thousand fantasies
Begin to throng into my memory,
Of calling shapes, and beck'ning shadows dire,
And airy tongues that syllable men's names
On sands and shores and desert wildernesses.
—John Milton, *Comus*

Like sands through the hourglass,
so are the days of our lives.
—*Days of our Lives*

CONTENTS

BRIDEFIGHT

Chapter 1

I wish I were dead.

It was 1:08 A.M. on the morning of September 17, and Lois Commoner was thinking thoughts that for her, of late, were typical.

As she was lying on the alley pavement, listening to the victim's broken sobbing, she thought, *Would I go to hell? No chance. This is hell. There's gotta be something else. And if there isn't, what do I have to lose?*

She banished such thoughts—now was *not* the time—and rolled over onto her stomach. She took a deep breath, put her palms flat on the filthy street, and pushed herself up until she was standing. This took six minutes and was just short of excruciating. Her knee was screaming. Her back had a kink in it. Her knuckles were bleeding. And she had a splitting headache. The headache bothered her more than anything else.

"I don't suppose you have any Advil in your pockets?" she asked the vic, who was crying and holding her purse strap. The purse itself was, of course, long gone. "Or even a Tylenol?" The victim had probably been a nice-looking woman when her evening began. Now the carefully coiffed blond hair was in disarray, her mascara was running down her cheeks, her dress was torn, and her shoulder probably hurt almost as much as Lois's knee. "How about just aspirin?"

The vic shook her head and kept crying. Lois's headache worsened. She considered telling the vic to cut the shit, then decided against it. She herself had become pretty jaded about this stuff, but that was no reason to be an unsympathetic jerk. At least not out loud.

Sirens wailed in the distance, which was a distinct relief. Blondie would be off her hands, and on some beat cop's. Well, that's what she—*they*—were paid for. Even better, the patrol unit would have aspirin.

"What happened?" Blondie finally asked. She held up her purse strap and stared at it like a betrayed lover. "Why didn't you stop him? Aren't you a cop? You told that—that *jerk* who took my purse you were a cop."

"Not anymore. I mean, I am, but I'm on desk duty now." Boy, did *that* admission taste bad. She actually spat to clear her mouth, then continued. "I got hurt a while ago. I'm off the streets." Her knee throbbed agreement, as if to say, *Damn right, chickie, and what'd you take off after him for, anyway? You must've known you couldn't have caught him. Couldn't resist playing hero again, sap?*

But it wasn't that simple. She'd seen someone in trouble, that was all. Heard the shriek and limped to the rescue. "Lois," her dad said before he choked to death on that Dorito, "boy, was that a bad choice for a name. You're nobody's sidekick, and you sure as shit never need rescuing."

That was then.

The black-and-white pulled up. She didn't recognize either of the officers who got out and approached them. They were as alike as two peas in a pod: both tall, stocky, and blond, with blue eyes—typical Minnesota stock. Lois, with her wild curly black hair and brown eyes, always felt like a gypsy among her Scandinavian coworkers.

"Good evening. I'm Officer Ristau, and this is my partner, Officer Carlson. Miss, do you need an ambulance? Either of you?"

"It's Detective Miss," she said, "and no. Just some Valium. Possibly some Percocets. But the vic would probably like an ambulance." *Or at least a shoulder to cry on.*

"He took my purse," Blondie said in a wounded voice. "My purse that my husband gave to me for Christmas. He took it. She tried to stop him and he took it anyway. My husband gave it to me."

She'd go on in this vein, Lois knew, for some time. Civilians were always utterly shocked when something unpleasant happened to them. They thought if they paid their taxes and didn't jaywalk and ate enough fiber, they were immune from mugging, rape, homicide, and intestinal trouble.

She envied them that surety.

While giving her statement, Lois studied the cop's sidearm and thought about death.

Chapter 2

How to do it? Pills? Jump off the IDS Tower? Stick the barrel of her Beretta in her mouth and pull the trigger? Watch the *Star Trek* marathon until she was brain dead? Eat all the leftovers in her fridge?

The gun, Lois decided, was not an option. Bad enough she was seriously considering the coward's way out; she wouldn't pervert her weapon by making it the instrument of her death. How many bad guys had she pointed it at? How many vics had she defended with it? How many hours had she spent on the shooting range, honing her skill to better serve her city? No, the gun was definitely out.

Pills were tempting. She had some excellent ones for her knee. Fifty of those, chased with a daiquiri or six, would probably do the job nicely. Add the Trekkie marathon to that and death was a certainty.

She got up from the couch, limped to her bathroom, grabbed the bottles out of the medicine cabinet, limped back, and lined them up like soldiers on her coffee table.

She looked at them thoughtfully. There wasn't much. She didn't believe in crutches, even when she had to use them to get down her front steps. As for pharmaceutical crutches, she hardly ever indulged. "Ballsy," her dad would have said. "Martyr," her mom would have sighed, shaking her head.

Well, they were both dead now. Following the Dorito Mishap, her mother had mourned for eight months, then made two decisions: to visit her sister in Saint Paul, and to fix her makeup at sixty-two miles an hour. The coroner hadn't been able to decide if she'd died from the impact of crashing into the back of the semi, or from the eyeliner (Revlon's Indigo Night) being driven into her right eye.

She didn't miss her father much, if truth be told. He'd been too big, too gruff, too disappointed she wasn't a boy, and toward the end, too drunk. Mostly she felt bad because he was dead, but she didn't feel too bad.

Her mother, though . . . that was a different story. Lois had felt adrift ever since her mother's death. When the one who bore you was gone, why bother with anything?

She shook off thoughts of her poor, doomed parents and returned her attention to the medication. There was a small bottle of OxyContin, the drug of choice for addicts—she'd busted a few OxyContin clinics in her day—a larger bottle of methadone, always popular with the chronic pain set, and a number of Duragesic patches.

She picked up one of the patches. How could she kill herself with these? Eat them? Stick a bunch around her heart?

And was she really, truly considering this? It sucked. It was the coward's way out. It defined her, forever, as a loser. The cops who found her after the neighbors called to report the smell would roll their eyes at each other. The coroner would roughly bundle her into a body bag. Her neighbors would shake their heads ("So quiet!" "Never a minute's trouble."), and her captain would be irritated. Her fellow detectives would be shocked that ballsy Lois Commoner had done such a thing, and would pity her, and would forget her.

She could feel a tear trickling down her left cheek, but made no move to wipe it away. Sure, it was a rotten thing to do, but what was the alternative? She'd been shot almost a year ago, and still woke to pain every morning. They'd never let her back on the streets. She'd been busted to desk officer, which meant she was one of the few secretaries in the city licensed to carry a firearm. Worst of all, she'd lost her shield.

The desk job was mindless, torturous, but she refused to take a medical retirement. *Then* what would she do? Sit around and try not to think about how badly her knee hurt? Real fulfilling.

And also you're so lone—

She shut that thought away, fast. That had nothing to do with anything.

There's got to be something else. Heaven. Hell. Reincarnation. Something. This isn't it, this can't be all there is. I didn't work so hard for so long to have this be the end of everything. There's something else out there, I know it.

And if she was wrong, if there was nothing, she'd take that over an unfulfilling life of pain and ennui.

She unbuttoned her shirt, then grabbed the remote and flicked it on to the Sci-Fi channel. Ah, there was Kirk talking to a doomed red-shirted security guard. Hour three of the marathon. She wondered what people who weren't suicidal were watching.

She took one of the Duragesic patches and stuck it to her chest, just above her bra. She did the same with the rest, then poured out the pills and looked at them. It was funny— they were so small, but they could stop her heart if she took enough of them. And she planned to swallow every one.

*If you do this, it's real. You'll be brain dead, followed by body
dead. You can't take it back.*

"God, I hope not," she said aloud, and went to plug in
the blender.

For the first time in forever, her knee didn't hurt. Nothing
hurt. She was floating—well, not really, she was still sitting
on the couch but she was also floating . . . floating and
watching McCoy chew Spock a new asshole . . . she spilled
her drink oh no red stain on the carpet . . . oh well . . . not
like she'd be around to care if she lost her security deposit . . .
Spock was logical . . . logical . . . logical to do this to end
this . . . it was all right . . . anything was better and she
couldn't . . . she couldn't . . . she couldn't . . . she was alone
and had nothing but the job . . . and now she didn't have the
job . . . so this was the only thing left to do . . . so she would
do it and if it made her a coward okay . . . and if it made her
a fool okay . . . as long as she wasn't lonesome anymore . . .
as long as it was all done over the end . . . *finito* . . . farewell . . .

Chapter 3

"**A**w, son of a *bitch!*"

Lois wasn't sure if she shouted it, or if it was just a thought. She could feel warm hands running over her limbs . . .

(checking for injury?)

. . . stroking her stomach, shoulders, even her breasts, and something warm and tickly on her lips, almost like a kiss, but of course that wasn't—

She was afraid to open her eyes and look. But she was afraid to keep lying there, too.

She wasn't dead. *Ergo,* she was alive. *Ergo,* she was in a hospital somewhere. *Ergo,* she'd have to go through Psych and treatment and T-groups and then try again sometime when they weren't watching her so carefully anymore. Dammit!

She opened her eyes. And instantly assumed the overdose had driven her insane.

She wasn't in a hospital. She wasn't even in her house. She was lying on the ground, in the middle of what looked like a desert—there was hard-packed sand everywhere, and one or two scrawny trees, and dunes in the distance. But it wasn't hot—it felt like a perfectly pleasant seventy-five degrees or so. And the light tickling on her lips was actually a raspy tongue. A puma was standing over her, and the sky was lavender. She wasn't sure which was more startling.

She blinked, then slowly rose to a sitting position. Yep, that was a purple sky, all right. She was in a desert that wasn't hot, and the sky was the color of an iris petal. She had definitely gone crazy. And the puma was backing off but still watching her. Her cheek still throbbed from its rough tongue.

She stared at the big cat, which was staring right back. It was enormous—probably two hundred and fifty pounds at least. Its coat was the color of the desert sand and—weird!—its eyes were the color of the purple sky. Its paws were huge, easily as big across as her hand if she spread her fingers wide.

It was sitting up very straight beside one of the stunted, twisted trees. Its tail—at least five feet long, and as thick around as her wrist—switched lazily back and forth. It seemed tame—it hadn't killed her in her sleep, after all.

She thought about standing up, rejected the idea, then reconsidered. After all, why was she being careful? She'd tried to commit suicide and now she was worried about a predator? What in God's name for?

She stood, slowly, never taking her eyes off the big cat. It was only when she was on her feet that she realized the last thing, the most shocking thing—her knee didn't hurt. Not even a tiny bit.

She flexed. She crouched. She jogged in place. Nothing, not a twinge, not a whimper.

"It worked!" she cried, forgetting herself for a moment. "I'm dead and—and somewhere else." Heaven? Hell? Some weird place in between? Who cared? She was out of pain for the first time in a long, long time. "I'm okay! I'm here and I'm okay! Do you hear? I made it and I'm okay!"

The puma was strolling toward her. She was so elated she

forgot to be afraid. "I'm better now," she told it. "Isn't that great?"

"*What was wrong with you?*" the puma asked. Except it didn't really speak—its jaws never moved. But she heard the question in her head.

After the purple sky and the painless limb, nothing was going to faze her. "Plenty of things, believe you me," she answered. "But I guess things are finally looking up." She cleared her throat. The puma was standing no more than two feet away, looking up at her. "You're—uh—not going to eat me, are you?"

"*I was thinking about it.*" Something was wrong with the cat's coat. It was shedding—no, its skin was rippling—no, it was sick—no, it was shrinking—no, it was growing—no, it was a man, a darkly tanned man with shoulder-length tawny blond hair and purple eyes. A man standing where the puma had just been. He grinned at her. His teeth were incredibly white and looked sharp. "Yes, I was definitely giving it some thought."

"*Aaaaaaaaaa—*"

"Are you all right?"

"*—aaaaaaaaaaaggggggggg—*"

"My lady? What's wrong?"

"*—gggggggggghhhhhhhhhhhhhhh—*"

"Um, well, I will just change back, then."

"*—hhhhhhhhhhhh—*what? No, don't do that. Just give me a minute." Panting, Lois sat down before she fell down. The puma man, who was splendidly nude, sat down cross-legged across from her. He was tanned, with the sleek muscles she had noticed before. His stomach was a washboard, and his forehead was creased with concern.

"Perhaps you need a healer," he suggested.

"Perhaps I need the department shrink, followed by several Budweisers. Um—what are you?"

"I am—a man, as you are a woman."

She snorted. The world—this strange new place—had stopped tilting, that was something. For a black moment, she'd thought she was going to faint. And that would be just too damned embarrassing. "Sure. Just a run-of-the-mill fella. Who can turn back and forth into a puma—"

"What is a poo-muh?"

"—and walks around naked and is magically delicious, besides."

"I know no magic."

"Never mind." She was trying not to stare, but couldn't help it. He was probably the best-looking guy she'd ever seen. He was big, but not bulky—his muscles had the lean definition of a swimmer's. His hair was gorgeous, tumbling around his shoulders, thick and wavy. His eyes were enormous, the palest lavender framed with darker purple lashes. His pubic hair, thank God, wasn't purple, but rather two shades darker than the hair on his head. His shoulders, legs, and arms were lightly furred, and his nails were longer than hers. Since she was a nail-biter, that wasn't much of a trick.

When they spoke, it was simultaneously.

"Where am I?"

"How did you come to be here?"

She laughed. "You first."

He smiled. She nearly flinched back, but restrained herself in time. His smile was much wider than a normal person's. She figured he had, at rough count, about a thousand teeth. "As you wish. This is my home. It is the SandLands. And you just appeared. Between one breath and the next, you appeared. I stayed, as I was curious. You slept for a long time."

"Well, thanks for not chomping me in my sleep."

He looked offended. "I would never."

"Oh, take it easy, I was only joking. As for your question,

I have no friggin' idea how I came to be here. I tried—back at my house, I was drinking a lot and—never mind. Anyway, I passed out and the next thing I knew, I was here."

"You must be a sorceress of unimaginable power."

"Ah—no. No, don't think so. I think being here was a big-ass accident. A good accident," she said hastily when his forehead creased again. "But it was nothing I did on purpose. Um—what next?"

"You will come with me to my home. I wish my father and brothers to meet you."

"Oh. Okay, then. Doesn't exactly sound like a request, though," she added in a mumble.

He rose in one fluid movement while she gaped in admiration, then extended his hand. It was almost twice as big as hers, and she wasn't exactly a shrimp.

She put her hand in his and let him pull her to a standing position. She sensed that he could have tossed her thirty feet if he wanted to. She tried not to stare below his waist, but couldn't resist peeking. He was long, thick, and semi-erect, which was flattering.

As if reading her mind, he looked down into her face and said matter-of-factly, "You are extremely beautiful."

She laughed at him. She hadn't meant to, but it was an absurd comment. She was built like a fire hydrant—dense and practical, but hardly the curvy, willowy blond specimen so popular in American society. She had no waist, and her legs were too long, and her tits were only so-so—she'd been a B cup for years. Plus, she had multiple scars from years of street scuffles—knife wounds, bullet wounds, even a permanent rope burn a junkie, high on acid and Jack Daniel's, had given her. Her hair was the nicest thing about her, and it was too curly, too wild, too out of control in humidity, and the color of a tar pit.

He put his hands on her shoulders and turned her around.

Even through her shirt, she could feel the heat from his hands, and his erection brushing against her back. This was alarming, yet delightful. She was facing the sun—a small, white orb—and in the distance she could see a castle.

"My home is there. May I keep you?" he asked, leaning down and speaking softly into her ear. She shivered and felt her entire left side erupt into goose bumps. She leaned back against him and felt him drop a kiss to the tip of her ear, then nuzzle the side of her neck. He was definitely an affectionate fellow, no doubt about that.

"Ah—nope. But I'd sure like to see where you live."

"As you wish, my lady. And about the other, we shall see." Before she could puzzle out what *that* was supposed to mean, his hands were abruptly gone, and when she turned to look at him, he was a puma again.

Out of pure curiosity, she stretched out her hands. Even when she put her hands thumb to thumb and spread her fingers wide, his head was still wider. He was truly enormous, bigger than any cat she'd ever seen on her own world. Even the lions on her world were smaller.

"My lady, what are you waiting for?" She could hear him laughing in her head. *"Mount, if you please."*

She blushed all the way down to her toes at the mental image that phrase conjured up, then awkwardly clambered on top of him with many grunts. "You mean I have to ride you to the castle-thingy?"

"Most citizens would say, 'O good lord, you mean I, your humblest servant, am allowed to ride atop you?'"

"Yeah, well, I'm not from around here, pally."

He laughed in her head again—God, that was so *weird!*—dug into the sand with all four paws, and they were off like a shot. She shrieked with surprise and joy and nearly fell off. She gripped him tighter with her knees and clutched his fur, which was coarse and soft at the same time—like rough silk. The stunted trees were whizzing by, his paws thudded into the hard-packed sand with the regularity of a metronome, and above her the lavender sky whirled and twirled. She laughed aloud and felt truly, deeply happy for the first time in a year.

"Oh, faster, can you go faster?" The wind was rushing in her face and the dust was making her eyes water and she was probably going to get a bloody nose if she let her face bang into his shoulder but she didn't give a tin-shit. All she knew was that she wasn't dead—or if she was dead, it was pretty swell—she wasn't in pain, and she was enjoying the first puma ride of her life with the most intriguing man she'd ever met. "Faster!"

She could hear the delight in his voice. *"Most ladies—and lords!—would be yetching all over my coat by now."*

"Yetching? You mean puking, barfing? Throwing up? Ha! I haven't thrown up since I was eight," she said scornfully. "And that was because I ate all our leftover Halloween candy."

"Hallo'een? You mean Spirit Night?"

"Hmm, *that's* interesting. Looks like your home and my home have some interesting parallels. And the reason I'm using words like 'interesting parallels' is because *you're not going fast enough."*

He snorted, then poured it on. She didn't talk anymore. She concentrated solely on hanging on. She had never been happier in her life.

Chapter 4

"That was something," she said, jumping off. She was panting from the adrenaline rush, but her knee didn't so much as squeak in pain. And she took fresh delight in that. "That was *really* something. Hey, gorgeous, maybe we can do it again sometime?"

He popped back to human form. It was still too quick for her eye to accurately report what happened when he transformed. "I am at my lady's command."

"Well, isn't that nifty. So, um—you live here?"

"Here" was the castle. When she'd seen it from the middle of the desert, it had looked like a small white castle dreaming in the distance. Up close it was, she figured, about the size of the Empire State Building. Except not as high. But it sure had the square footage of Manhattan real estate. She had to tip her head *waaaaaaay* back to see the top of the spires.

It looked just like the castles she'd seen pictures of back home, except it was pure, dazzling white. She assumed they had mined the stone from a nearby quarry . . . about a thousand years ago. The flags flying atop the spires were brightly colored and had animals on them—she spotted a puma atop all the others, but lions, leopards, and even a few house cats were also represented.

There were several people about, going to and from the castle, and every one of them was staring at her as they hurried by. She assumed it was her clothes—or her coloring, because they were, to a man, woman, and child, all blond. And they sure weren't wearing an old workout bra and tattered gym shorts. Shit, she was practically as naked as puma-man was. Somewhere along the way, her old shirt had disappeared.

There were dozens of shades of blond represented, from the fairest platinum to what her dad had always called "dirty dishwater blond." And while many of them had wavy locks, none of them sported a headful of wild curls, as she did.

Ah, great . . . dead and *a freak. Perfect.*

". . . all my life."

"Huh?"

"I said, in answer to your question, that I have lived in the Castle Royale all my life."

"Oh, right. Sorry, I forgot the question. Is that why they're staring at me instead of you? I mean, at least *I'm* wearing clothes."

"I told you," he said simply. "You are beautiful, and so they stare."

"Uh-huh." She changed the subject. "So, are you going to give me the nickel tour, or what? After you get dressed," she added in a mutter.

His brow wrinkled. "Uh . . . yes. Might I first have your name, good lady?"

"Right! I can't believe I forgot about that."

"You are increasingly forgetful, it seems," he teased.

She grinned back. As long as he was standing here, talking to her, she didn't mind the stares so much. "Today, yes. I'm Lois Commoner."

She stuck out her hand. He looked at it and didn't say anything.

"*Helloooooo?*" She waved her hand in front of his face. "And you are?"

"Please forgive; I was waiting to hear your rank and affiliations."

"Oh, as to that—well, up 'til yesterday, it was Detective Lois Commoner, Minneapolis Police Department."

"That is an odd affiliation."

"Well, it worked for me, once upon a time."

He took her still-proffered hand, and seemed unsure of what to do with it. Finally he patted it, then let it go. "I am Damon."

"Is that Demon or Damien? 'Cuz I got problems with both."

"Day-MAWN."

"Oh." He stuck out his hand and she shook it firmly. He watched their hands pump up and down, bemused. "It's nice to meet you. Thanks again for the ride."

"You have but to ask if you desire another one. Come, I would like you to meet my father."

He hadn't let go of her hand that time; instead he pulled her through the gigantic doorway, into the castle's, er, yard, or whatever it was called. But before they could get very far, a short blond woman wearing what looked like a leather tunic and pants came racing toward them. Lois didn't have a chance to see what she looked like before she skidded in the dirt before them, then hit the ground with her arms stretched over her head.

"Forgive my impertinence, Prince Damon!" she cried into the dirt. "His Majesty the King has been asking for you all morning."

"Of course. Thank you, Rejar."

Damon charged for the inner door, pulling Lois so hard

she actually lost her feet. "Whoa! Slow down. Or leggo and I'll follow you."

"Forgive—I will be right back. Remain here, if you please." With that he dropped her hand and was through the door in a half second.

She rubbed her wrist—he hadn't meant to hurt her, but the marks of his fingers remained—and stared at everyone staring at her.

Two choices: hang out here and be gawked at, or follow Damon. Prince *Damon. Did she say* Prince?

She followed.

It wasn't difficult to track Damon down. She followed the shouting. Two floors and five halls later, she figured out what the problem was. It seemed the king—Damon's dad?— was as sick as a dog, and everybody was yelling at everybody else about what to do about it. From the fuss, these guys didn't get sick very often.

She peeked through the doorway—no doors that she had seen, just large archways that led from one room to another. The archways were tall—at least seven feet high—and so wide, four of her could have gone through them at once.

She could see Damon and two other men standing around yelling. Well, they weren't exactly yelling—they were sort of politely disagreeing with each other very loudly. At least Damon had put some clothes on—he was wearing a robe several shades lighter than his hair, with a blazing sun embroidered on the front.

"—all respect to my good lordly brother—"

"—helping our good father the king by—"

"—turn a slops bucket o'er my good lordly brother's tiny head—"

"—try it, my good tiny brother—"

"—both of you should grow headfirst in a pile of Stinkweed, beloved princes—"

Others—she assumed they worked in the castle, as they weren't dressed nearly as nicely as Damon's brothers— were surrounding Damon and the men, and occasionally trying to get a word in edgewise.

She walked down to the next room and peeked inside. And gasped—what a room!

She'd seen a picture of the queen's chambers at Buckingham Palace once. This room put Queen Elizabeth's digs to shame.

It was enormous—the ceiling was at least twenty feet high, and the room itself was as big as the entire Homicide Department. Windows had been cut into the stone near the top of each wall, and the floor was splashed with pale lavender sunlight.

A professional football team could have comfortably slept in the bed, but there was only one person in it now—a man whose blond hair was liberally sprinkled with gray. He looked to be in his late fifties, and his complexion had a definite greenish tinge. He was huddled under richly embroidered blankets—only his head was showing—and looked as unhappy as a junkie in withdrawal.

He groaned in abject misery, which made up her mind. She cautiously approached the bed and cleared her throat.

"Hi there," she said. His eyes—the same pale purple as Damon's—opened wide and he stared at her, stunned. "Can I get you something? Some Pepto-Bismol? A bucket? You look like you're gonna—"

He groaned again, lurched upright, and threw up all over her.

"—be sick," she finished. She stood there, dripping, and contemplated him. "Something you ate?" she asked at last.

He nodded and slumped back against the filthy bed-clothes. "That I should so dishonor a lady, and one who came to me out of a need to lend aid!"

"Chill out, I'll live. You know, you'd be a lot more comfortable with clean sheets. And wouldn't you like some soup? Like—uh—chicken broth? Do they have chickens here? Do they have broth, even? Never mind, I'll find out. And aren't you thirsty? If you're gonna be this sick, you should drink a lot. Don't go away," she added.

She turned, and saw several people—Damon among them—standing in the huge doorway. "Yeah, there you are—listen, I'm going to need clean sheets, and some cold water—can you do ice water?—and some broth. Light stuff, nothing heavy. Maybe a little bread, if you have some. *No* butter . . . no dairy products at all. Oh, and someone better find me an old shirt or something to run around in. Don't suppose there's a washing machine in the basement?"

Nobody moved.

"Hey! I'm talking to you people!" She marched up to the doorway and made shooing gestures. "Get your asses in gear, the old guy's pretty miserable."

"You cannot be here," one of the servants finally ventured, eyes rolling like a scared horse. "This area is for royalty and the servants of same. You—"

"—seem to be the only one *doing* something."

"Do as she commands," Damon said suddenly. Beside him, two other muscular blonds—his princely brothers?—were smiling at her.

"Well, *thank* you."

"But 'the old guy' is His Majesty the King! She cannot—"

"I don't give a shit if he's the Pope. He's hurting, and you dildos are just standing around. Now *move*." She put her hand on the nearest chest—it was Damon's—and shoved. Then she noticed the heavy curtain beside the doorway, and tugged on it. It fell into place, obscuring everyone from sight, with a satisfying flap.

From behind the heavy curtain, she heard a plaintive, "What is a dildo?," and then many retreating footsteps.

"Come here," the king said weakly.

She turned and stomped back to the bed. "Sorry about that, but Jesus! Someone had to light a fire under those guys."

"My name is not Jesus. But you do such things very well. Sit here beside me. Ah—your clothing will be tended to, and I must again humbly implore your forgiveness for my foul and coarse behavior—"

"Don't worry about it. You wouldn't believe how many times I've been puked on, spit on, had shit flung at my head, not to mention bullets—seriously, this is nothing. Shoot, I've had dates that weren't this pleasant."

"The lady is too kind. If you will permit a bold query, does your striking coloring come from your sire or your dam?"

"Um . . . my mom's Black Irish, if that's what you mean."

"I do not know that tribe. I *would* know all about how you came to my home." He leaned back against the pillows and wriggled to get comfortable. He looked happy for the first time since she came into the room.

Poor guy's probably bored to death. Not used to staying in bed, that's for damn sure.

"Sure, I'll talk. What do you want to know?"

"I do beg you to tell me everything, good lady."

"Your son—Damon?—brought me. My name's Lois, by the way."

"I am Sekal, Lord High King of the SandLands, Ruler of the Exalted Ranges of the OnHigh Mountains, Emperor of the Snowy Islands, Maker of the—"

"So, Sekal, yeah, nice to meet you." She automatically

stuck her hand out, then cursed herself as he just looked at it. She sort of waved at him and continued. "As to how I got here . . ." She started to talk. She was still talking when tight-lipped servants showed up with fresh nightgowns—one for her, one for the king—sheets, blankets, and food.

While the servants bustled around, changing sheets and offering her clothes, the king beckoned and Damon was instantly at his side. He started to kneel, but the king waved weakly and Damon took his hand instead. "Ho, my son, when you said you left to go a-hunting, I did not think you should enjoy so much luck!"

"Nor I, my good father."

"And at exactly the right time, too."

"Yes, Father."

"Right time for what?" Lois asked, but then she was hustled behind a changing divider, and being divested of her clothes. She slapped the servant's hands away. "I can undress myself, thanks. What's your name?"

"Zeka, my lady."

Zeka—poor kid, what a moniker!—was a petite woman with curly blond hair and the greenest eyes Lois had ever seen. They were the color of a newly mown lawn, and as big as quarters. She was dressed simply in a white robe—in fact, all the servants were dressed in white, draped robes; they looked like escapees from the set of *Gladiator*.

"Well, Zeka, whatcha got there?"

Teeny Zeka was hefting a brimming stone jug—the thing had to weigh thirty pounds!—with one arm, and pouring bluish-purple water into a large basin. A delightful perfumed scent rose from the splashing water; a cross between roses and water lilies. Suddenly Lois wanted a bath. Very badly.

"If you would be so good as to hand me your soiled

clothes, I will see them washed. In the meantime, if you approve, you may wear this." She held up a plain white robe.

"Sure, looks great. Thanks a lot." Lois quickly stripped down to nothing, feeling a little awkward. She would have preferred to keep her panties, but all her clothing stank. Working quickly, she sponged herself clean with the water and rough towel Zeka provided. She turned to slip into the robe when Zeka gasped.

"You—you have many, *many* battle marks!"

"Uh, yeah. Also known as hideous scar tissue. Thanks for noticing—*and* yelling about it." Lois knew her body wasn't exactly a candidate for a *Playboy* pullout. "Jeez, calm down, willya?"

But Zeka was already darting out of the small changing space. She heard urgent whispers and grabbed for the robe, about two seconds too late. Suddenly the divider was wrenched aside, and Damon and his brothers were standing there.

"Jesus Christ!"

"By the Great Lion," one of the brothers whispered. "What a woman!"

The other brother reached out and touched the puckered bullet scar above her right breast. She smacked his hand away with her fist and clutched the robe to her chest. "Hands off, unless you want to spit out your teeth," she snapped. The prince's eyebrows arched as she continued. "You guys might be comfortable walking around without any clothes on, but I'm an old-fashioned girl."

"Things are different here," Damon said mildly, his gaze riveted to the rope burn on her shoulder.

"Thanks for the news flash. Now buzz off so I can get dressed!"

"What is it?" the king called weakly. "What is the matter?"

"Nothing, Father," Damon said. "Our visitor is simply more beautiful than any of us had imagined."

"Lord, what has that boy been smoking?" Lois muttered. One of the brothers edged forward, staring at the knife scar near her belly button, but she kicked out at him, effectively herding him back. The other brother laughed. "Get lost. Go find some other woman to ogle."

"Oooh-gull?"

"Stare at. Gape. Gawk."

"I must beg a lady's pardon, but your beauty robbed us of—"

"Yeah, yeah."

"—our good manners. I am Maltese, second in line to the throne of the SandLands, Prince of the—"

"Fine, I'm Lois, nice to meet you."

The other blond—they were as alike as twins, except this one had eyes the deep green of wet leaves, while Maltese's eyes were the color of the sea after a winter storm. "I am Shakar, third in line to the—"

"Meetcha. You mind turning around while I put this on?"

"I do mind, yes."

"I also."

She almost grinned. They hadn't sounded like sarcastic jerks, just honest. "Fine, I'll turn." She did, and heard an exhalation of breath come from someone. What now? Were they admiring the dimples on her ass? Christ!

"How did my lady come here?"

"To make a long story short, Damon gave me a ride."

Zeka gasped. "But the royal family never—"

"Zeka," Maltese said reprovingly. "What our good brother does is none of our concern . . . usually."

"Forgive, my good prince."

When she turned back, Damon was shooing his brothers away with helpful punches to their shoulders. She opened her mouth but he cupped her chin in one hand, effortlessly stifling her outburst. "I believe I requested you stay in the courtyard," he said solemnly, but his eyes crinkled at the corners in a friendly way.

"What am I, your dog? 'Sit, Lois. Stay.' *Shyeah!* Besides, I don't like being left by myself," she added in a grumble.

"Then I shall endeavor to be at your side at all times."

"Uh—that's not exactly what I—"

"Lois! My good son!"

"Just a *minute, we're talking.* Jeez, sick people, I swear to God. Now, listen, Damon, I gotta figure out about a zillion things, here, like where I'm gonna stay, and—"

"With me."

"Uh. Okay, that's very nice and all, but—"

"Put her in the chambers beside mine," the king called.

Lois thought that was awfully nice of him, but the effect on Damon was dramatic: his eyes went narrow and flinty and he actually snarled, *snarled*, like one big pissed-off cat. Puma. Whatever.

He spun around and stalked back to the king's bed. "What be you thinking, my good king who will be my dead king if he tries to take my prize?"

"Peace, my son. The lady needs a chamber appropriate to her station . . . whatever that will be. And we have agreed those rooms would suit that station, yes?"

"Uh . . . yes."

"Those rooms have been empty too long. As to the other matter," the old king added coolly, a tone that caused Damon to flush and drop his eyes, "I have not decided."

"What? What does that mean? What's everyone talking about? Can I get a translator or something? Hey, get your ass back in bed!" She walked over and gave the king a gentle push. He seized her arm with surprising strength, and Lois found herself pulled forward onto the king's giant bed, with an old man who was as strong as an ox staring right into her eyes. "Listen, buster, I'm all for respecting your elders, but you've got about half a second to—"

"Peace, Lady Lois. I only wished to catch the full effect of your scent." He sniffed her hair. "Feh! You smell much like my yetch, despite your washup. Damon, see that she gets a proper bath. Lois, when you are clean, come back and tell me more of your world. I wish to hear more about 'the IA pricks and the dumb-ass political games.' "

"After you eat your soup," she said firmly.

"The child knows our station and yet dares to give the king orders! Well, 'twould not kill me to obey, instead of being obeyed. It will be as you wish, Lois. But you must stay for a long time and tell many stories."

Despite Damon's frown, she agreed.

Chapter 5

"**D**amn!"
"Is something wrong?"

"Hardly." Lois stared at the bathing room. It was about half the size of the king's chambers, which meant it was the largest bathroom in the galaxy. Instead of a tub, there was a pool in the middle of the room, and from the perfume in the air, it was more of that delicious bathing water Zeka had poured for her. Big bunches of white flowers—the blooms were as big as her fist—floated in the pool. They looked like fluffy orchids. There were several marble countertops scattered about the room, and two people were getting massages.

"May I bathe with you, Lady Lois?"

"Uh—" *No way. Buzz off. I usually take baths by myself. I doubt I'll be able to keep my hands off you, so for your own safety . . .* "Sure." Given that there were at least half a dozen people in the room, she wasn't worried about her virtue—not that she had any to worry about. Besides, he'd opened up his home to her, and she would have a place to sleep, at least for tonight. To refuse—especially when this society seemed so open about public nudity—would be churlish, to say the least.

Still, it wasn't every day she stripped in front of strangers.

She got out of her robe as quickly as possible, tossed it on a countertop, and stepped down into the pool. She heard a gasp of appreciation behind her and rolled her eyes. What *was* it with these people? They clearly had her confused with Pamela Anderson.

The water was deliciously warm, and she sank into it up to her chin. She couldn't help groaning appreciatively as the perfumed water soothed her all over. "Oh, *man*, this is the life."

"Indeed."

She whipped around; Damon had managed to come up right behind her without her hearing him. "Jeez, don't do that! I swear I'm hanging a bell around your neck."

He smiled at her and plucked a flower out of the water. "If it pleases you. Now, you will allow me . . . ?"

She cautiously approached him, and he plunked the flower on top of her head. While his fingers were busily working through her hair, she realized the flower's petals were disintegrating into a kind of soap.

His fingers were marvelously strong, and she resisted the urge to melt against him. This was probably the best day of her life—and she'd been here only three hours! She knew she should be fretting—she'd started the day planning to be dead, after all. She knew she should be thinking about how to get home, or at least worrying about her future. This place couldn't be as great as it seemed. It just couldn't. But all she wanted to do was let Damon rub her all over, then take a nap.

"You are *sooooooo* good at that."

"Thank you. It is a true pleasure to attend to my lady's needs." Now he was washing her breasts, working the sudsy petals all over her skin, paying special care to her nipples, which instantly swelled and started to ache.

What's wrong with me? I'm letting a stranger feel me up in a public bathhouse! And it feels really, really good.

She batted his hands away, and he obligingly drew her closer and began working the suds into her back. She was pressed against his broad chest and could feel his erect length pressing into her stomach.

Thank goodness it's a public bath, or who knows what I'd let this guy do.

"Um." She turned her face so her cheek was resting against his nipple. It was either that, or give in to the urge to lick it. "Thanks for letting me stay here. I s'pose I should figure out where to go tomorrow, or at least—"

"Later," Damon said firmly, still stroking her back.

"Works for me," she sighed. One of the flowers floated by and she grabbed it. "Here, let me return the favor." She pulled back, rubbed it over his chest, and watched in fascination as the leaves crumbled into a sweet-smelling foam. "What's this stuff called?"

"These are *beriblooms.*"

"Well, they're great. I could ship a crate to Mary Kay, make a fortune."

"Is Mary Kay as lovely as you?" He kissed the corner of her mouth at the same time she felt his hands slide over her buttocks and rub, rub, rub.

"Um . . . what?"

"Mary Kay."

His fingers were kneading her flesh, and she had to fight the urge to grab his cock.

"What about Mary Kay?"

"What?"

"Um."

"Ah."

She was reaching for what she craved when . . .

"Oh ho, good brother!"

She looked up and saw the other two princes standing by the pool. The smaller one—"smaller" meaning he was only five inches taller than she, as opposed to seven—was kneeling by the pool, dabbling his fingers in the water. The taller one—was it Maltese? What, was that as in falcon?—was standing with his arms crossed over his chest. She jerked back from Damon, feeling her face grow hot from mortification.

"Now, my good lordly brother, you must give everyone a chance," Maltese chided.

"No I must not," Damon replied cheerfully. He reached out and pulled Lois back against his soapy chest. She wriggled, but he had a grip like iron.

"It should be an interesting sunrise, then," Shakar said, grinning. "Even more so if Father joins in."

Damon lost his smile, not to mention his hard-on. "You don't think—?"

"No. Still, he is our good lord, and his will is the will of the SandLands, so who knows?"

"I wish you guys would tell me what you're talking about," she said irritably. Then, to Damon, "Leggo."

"Tomorrow is the Bridefight," Shakar explained. "Many, many royals and nobles will come to battle for mates. The winner gets first choice of the ladies. The second-winner gets second choice, and so on. This happens once every three sunrounds, so it is our great good luck that you are visiting."

"Oh. Say, you're not kidding. That sounds kind of interesting. Can I watch?"

"You are the guest of honor," Damon whispered in her ear, which made her shiver.

"Quit that. Great! I'd sure like to see it. Uh—you guys don't battle to the death or anything, do you?"

"Hardly ever," Maltese said after a pause.

Shakar considered for a long moment, then gave her what he probably thought was a reassuring smile, showing only about six hundred teeth. "No one has perished in many, many sunrounds."

"Of course, when there is a new element—"

"Tempers flare."

"But all will probably be well."

"The three of you can stop teasing me any second now," she said irritably. "Really, you're like a bunch of kids."

"Goats?"

"Children."

"Ah! Cubs!"

"*Anyway.* I'm clean enough. And so are you," she told Damon, who tried to grab her again, but slick as an eel, she slipped away. "Can someone show me where I'm s'posed to sleep?"

Maltese and Shakar tussled so hard for the privilege, it was an easy matter for Damon to boot them into the pool, and escort Lois to her sleeping chambers.

Lois peeked in on the king, who was asleep. "I'll come back tomorrow morning," she whispered to Damon.

"I will tell him, if he is wakeful."

"Thanks."

He brought her to the next chamber, which was as large as the king's, except with softer colors—moss greens and tans and pinks.

"Holy cow!" She added in a whisper, "Are you sure I'm supposed to sleep here?"

The two servants—the room was so big she hadn't noticed them right away—jumped to attention. "Good even, my lady!" one of them—it was Zeka—said. "If it is your will, we will help you retire."

"Would my lady like a bedsnack ere she retires?" The

other servant, a short, stocky man with reddish blond hair and a goatee, stepped forward with a covered tray.

"A bedsn—yeah, sounds great. A sandwich would be perfect."

"We have pupoons, graldens, and derslangs."

Pupoons turned out to be fruit that tasted like a strawberry mated with a pear, except it had blue, pebbly skin. *Graldens* were delightfully chewy nuts that put hazelnuts to shame—and you could eat the shells, too! *Derslangs* were tiny little biscuits that tasted like they'd been smothered in honey and butter, and baked until tender.

"No more," Lois groaned sometime later. "Cripes, I'm so full I'm gonna puke. And I think there's been enough of that for one day."

"Good eve," Damon said to the servants, who cleaned up the platters and quickly left.

"Say, they had a major attitude adjustment," Lois commented, sitting on the bed. "When I was helping your dad, I thought they were gonna hit me."

"Mmmm."

"You didn't—uh—say anything, did you?"

"No. My father did . . . when he gave you the queen's chambers."

She blinked. "The queen's?"

"My departed mother's," he said simply. "She took a bedfever when our sister was born, and perished. My sister did not wish to be a babe without her dam, and quickly followed her to the Place of Spirits."

"I'm sorry. That sucks."

"Yes. It sucked quite a lot."

"How old were you when it happened?"

"I had sixteen sunrounds."

"That's really rotten. Both my parents are dead, but at least I got to grow up first."

"It would seem we have a great deal in common."

"Yeah, sure." *Not.* She changed the subject. "It was nice of your dad to give me your mom's room, but do you think it's okay? I mean, this is *the queen's bedroom.* I'm a nobody. I can't even get a Gold Card back home."

"The king's will is our will."

"Still." But she shrugged and climbed under the covers. The bed was delightfully soft and she sank into it a good eight inches. "*Ahhhhhhh,* I could get used to this."

"That is good."

"What?"

He bent over her. It was so creepy, the way he could cross a room without making a sound. "Good even, my lady." He kissed her on the forehead, like a brother.

"Night, Damon. Thanks again for everything today."

He kissed her on the cheek like a brother.

"Uh—good night."

He kissed her on the mouth, not remotely like a brother. His tongue swept inside and his hand was on the back of her neck—hard, possessive. She figured she should kick or gouge or something, but he smelled great and he was un-believably gorgeous and, hey, he was a prince, too. What the fuck.

She kissed him back. She rubbed her tongue against his and clutched his shoulders, which were thrumming with strain. He made a noise, deep in his throat, quite like a growl, and then she was tugging him toward her.

"Don't just stand there," she growled. "Tuck me in."

"It is forbidden," he said soberly. "You are an honored lady and guest." Still, he was climbing under the sheets with her. "Also, you are an excellent wine."

"Thanks. You've got some pretty good mojo yourself going on, Damon." This was difficult to say without breath-ing hard, as his hands were stroking over her breasts, her stomach, and were now easing her thighs apart. "You'd . . . uh . . . better get lost before I do something *really* crazy." *Killing myself was nutty enough.* "I don't want you to get into trouble."

"Well. There are ways and ways." She couldn't see him anymore; he had ducked beneath the covers. She could feel his mouth close over one of her nipples, and she groaned. His mouth—and his body!—were a few degrees warmer than hers, and he felt like the most sensual electric blanket ever imagined.

"Sure, but also, I'm not the kind of girl who fucks on a first date. Not that we've been on a date," she added breathlessly as he licked the cup of her bellybutton. "But you know what I mean."

"I do not." She could barely hear him; he was muffled against her flesh. "But I will find out."

She put her hands on his shoulders, marveling at the firm feel of his muscles beneath her palms. Then he ducked lower, and she felt his thumbs on her cunt, parting her, and then felt him take a long, slow lick.

She nearly leapt off the bed. His tongue was raspy and felt utterly, unbelievably delightful. He licked her like a cat lapping up a bowl of cream, and she squirmed around to offer him better access. Her legs were spread so wide she was practically doing the splits. She could hear what sounded like a throaty growl . . . then she realized he was purring, purring while he licked and sucked and licked some more.

When his tongue rasped over her clit again and again, she crammed her fist against her lips—mindful of the king sleeping next door—and groaned wildly against her fingers. Her uterus clenched and she felt waves of pleasure race down her limbs as she came . . . and came . . . and came.

He crawled back up and she reached down, groped for

his cock, and stroked the delicious long velvety length. His eyes rolled up as she tightened her grip and pumped, and in a matter of seconds she could feel him spurting.

"Good thing we didn't actually have sex," she chortled as he collapsed over her. "Ew. Don't even think about making me sleep on the wet spot."

"I will have servants change the bedclothes," he groaned.

"No, forget it. It's late. Besides, this bed is huge. I'll just slide six feet over and sleep there."

"Perhaps I will, also."

"Perhaps you should get your ass back to your own bed." Mutual coming was one thing, but she wasn't about to actually *sleep* with a near-stranger. She did have some standards.

He groaned again and stood, then staggered toward the doorway. "I leave you then, my Lady Lois of the Magical Fingers."

"As a nickname, that leaves a lot to be desired." Her eyelids were already drooping. It had been a helluva day.

"Until tomorrow, Lady Magical Fingers." He grinned at her and left, closing the door curtain behind him.

She slept deeply, sweetly . . . and without pain.

Chapter 6

The next morning, servants woke her up, dressed her in gorgeous flowing robes the color of cherry Kool-Aid, and escorted her down one floor, where Damon and Maltese were waiting. Her new clothes, she noticed, were quite a bit nicer than the simple white robe the servants had offered her yesterday. That was a troubling thought, but she determinedly pushed it away. Nothing was going to spoil this, her first full day in a new land.

"Good morn, my lady!"

"Hi, Maltese. Hi, Damon." She practically blushed looking at him, remembering last night all too well. And from the way he was looking at her, he was thinking the same thing she was.

"You slept well?" he asked politely, but his gaze was so hot, it nearly scorched her.

"Slept *great*. Is it breakfast time? Is that where you guys are going?"

"A lady with a fine appetite," Maltese said approvingly. "That is good."

"You should have seen all the *derslangs* she devoured last even," Damon teased. "I admit I feared to approach too closely."

"Great. Puma comedians."

"Nearly all is in readiness for the fights today," Damon explained as they walked her down the corridor. "Your place has been chosen; once you have broken fast, we will take you there. We must then prepare ourselves."

"Okay. Thanks again for the ringside seat. Is this an okay thing to wear today?"

"You look beautiful," Maltese assured her. "You are a visitor, so no one expects to see your rank badges or affiliations."

"I do have a badge, though. I mean, I did. I guess my old shield would be the closest thing to an affiliation. Jeez, I sure wish my footlocker was here."

"Your what?"

"My footlocker . . . it's this big metal box that I kept at the foot of my bed. Most women have hope chests, I've got my dad's old army footlocker. Anyway, it had some old clothes, and my shield, a bunch of my guns, and some ammo, too." She shrugged and turned. "Oh, well, no use crying over—ow!" Lois suddenly ended up on the floor.

She'd tripped over something. Something that hadn't been there five seconds ago. She looked over her shoulder and saw her footlocker.

Damon leaned down. "Are you going to make that noise again?"

"*Aaaaaagggggggggggg*—"

"I take it this is your footlocker?"

"*—gggggggggghhhhhhhhhh!*"

Damon helped her up. She reared back and gave her footlocker a kick—yep. Solid as a rock. This was no hallucination. "Someone better tell me *what the fuck is going on!*"

"I told you," Damon said patiently, though the corner of his mouth twitched upward. "You are a powerful sorceress.

You have but to call what you need out of the air, and it comes."

"It has happened before," Maltese added.

"*What?* You mean other people have just sort of popped up, and they wish out loud for things, and then their shit shows up, too?"

". . . yes. If I understand you correctly."

"Do not count on it," Damon chortled.

"Jeez, why didn't any of you *say* something? So I could— I could wish myself home, if I wanted?"

Damon looked distinctly alarmed, and now Maltese was the one fighting a smile. "Peace, my good brother—as to your question, fair Lois, yes, you could wish yourself home. But not for much longer. The ability only lasts for a few sunsets. Then you will remain with us until the end of your days."

"Oh."

"There was no need to tell her that," Damon said sulkily.

"Shame, my good prince. To keep things from a lady so as to not have an interruption to your pleasures."

Damon flushed, but she was barely paying attention. Things were getting—she could hardly believe it was possible—weirder and weirder. There must be a portal or something, a doorway between her world and theirs, and when someone from Earth was near death, they could get through it. Or something. Shit, what did she know? She'd never read so much as a single sci-fi book in her life. Truc crime was more her literary bag. "Well, that's—interesting. I guess."

"You will not," Damon said firmly. "You will not wish yourself away."

"And if I do?" she teased.

"Then I will gag you until your ability has flown."

"Careful," she warned, though she felt a tingle at his

silly-ass possessiveness. "My footlocker's here now, with all my guns. Mind I don't shoot off your kneecap."

"That does sound unpleasant," he admitted. "I do not wish you to do that."

"Has anyone ever gone back?"

"No. Never. I would be . . . displeased . . . should you be the first."

"Hmm." She lapsed into silence. So no one had gone back—they'd killed themselves or died while desperately unhappy and woken up in a land of shapeshifters and uncommon courtesy, a land where the weather was sunny and seventy-five degrees, where the royal family was worshipped but the commoners had it pretty good, too. Where strangers were welcomed and wooed. No fucking wonder no one had gone back.

The question was, would she be the first?

And why was she even considering it?

She really did have the best seat in the house. It was right next to the king's chair, which was conspicuously empty. Servants practically fought for the privilege of bringing her treats, and before the Bridefight had even started, Lois was stuffed.

Still, she kept eating. She picked another squashy, milk-chocolate-colored sweetmeat out of the brimming bowl Zeka was holding for her. "What are these things?"

"*Kumkoss,* my lady."

"Well, they taste like the hybrid of a Tootsie Roll and a marshmallow. Yum! Say, it's kind of making me nervous, the way you hover over me all the time. Why'n't you sit down, take a load off?"

Zeka looked alarmed. "I could not, my lady."

"It's Lois, and sure you can. Just have a seat."

"You are kind, but I must not. Look! They begin."

Still chomping, Lois looked. The place really was like something out of *Gladiator* ... the arena was all hard-packed sand and blinding white, almost too white to look at. The tanned fighters stood out dramatically against it. They were, naturally, naked and, interestingly, not a few of them were aroused. Thinking about picking their future brides, maybe? She couldn't help but notice there wasn't a teeny weenie in the bunch. Lois finally quit trying to avert her eyes—there were about twenty naked guys running around the arena floor, too many to avoid looking at—and settled back to enjoy the show.

Still, irritating thoughts kept intruding. Like, *If I killed myself here, would I wake up back on Earth? Or would I be dead-for-real? And why am I thinking about this morbid shit? Jeez!*

The fighters were announced one by one. Interestingly, they all trotted up to her seat and bowed when their names were called. She waved back. These guys really knew how to treat a visitor! And they all looked like escapees from a Mr. Hardbody calendar. Not a scrawny, short fella in the bunch.

When Damon came, she tossed him a *kumkoss*, which he snatched out of the air and popped in his mouth so quickly, she never saw his arm move. "A boon from my lady!" he called triumphantly, and the crowd cheered.

"It's candy, not a boon," she told him, but he was already moving back to his place, his gorgeous backside flexing as he walked. She nearly fell out of her seat as she craned to get a last look at that fine butt before he turned again.

There was dead silence when the last name—King Sekal—was called. She saw Maltese's and Shakar's mouths pop open in surprise, but Damon just frowned.

"Have a care, my good lord," he said in the abrupt silence.

The king, who had just finished bowing to her, grinned. "Shalt take your own advice, my good son?"

Meanwhile, Zeka and two other servants were fighting so hard over who would be the one to pour Lois a drink, her beverage ended up on the floor. "Cut it out, you guys," she said, turning around and giving the three of them a good glare. "Go find somebody else to bug."

"But my lady is the one . . . one we wish to . . . bug!"

"Too bad. Go on, shoo."

She turned back to watch the action—and nearly shrieked. The king and his opponent had just . . . *transformed.* The king was a puma, like Damon, except leaner and longer, with a gray face. His opponent was a black leopard.

The fight happened so quickly, before she knew it, it was over. The puma and the leopard fought, were men again, slugged it out as men, were animals again, clawed and bit, and now they were punching, and now they were leaping, and now they were kicking, and now the king was bowing to her in man-form and the leopard was rolling over on its back, showing throat. It happened so fast, she was shocked, frozen. Finally, she clapped. It seemed the polite thing to do. After a long beat, the audience followed her, awkwardly banging their hands together.

These guys are sooooo polite, Lois thought. *They put "Minnesota nice" to shame.*

This went on with surprising rapidity. Lois wasn't sure if they were letting the king win because he was the king, or because the old guy was a righteous ass-kicker. Regardless, it was a helluva show.

He beat Maltese. He beat Shakar. And when it seemed the entire arena was holding its collective breath, when Damon grimly approached him for a turn, the king abruptly bowed to Damon, bowed to her, and walked off the field with dignity to spare.

The crash of applause was thunderous; she nearly jumped out of her skin. By now, the audience had gotten used to clapping, even enjoyed it, and they gave the king what he had earned, and then some. Minutes later, he was settling into his seat beside hers.

"Awesome," she told him.

"My lady humbles me."

"Didn't want to puncture Damon's ego, huh?"

"My point was made, I think, and I am too old for such games. Still," he added wistfully, taking her hand in his, "it was enjoyable while it endured. I'truth, my lady, I doubt I would have beaten my eldest. Best not to let him find out for sure."

She laughed, and after a moment, the king joined in.

Once the king had dropped out, the pecking order was quickly established. And before another hour had passed, Damon had been proved the winner, with Maltese in second place and Shakar in third. Lois clapped hard. The royal family had certainly kicked ass and taken names today! She could really get behind a family like that.

"The winner, ruler of the Bridefight, with first choice of mate . . . our good Prince Damon!"

"What's he doing now?" Lois asked, puzzled, as Damon darted toward her then, with one bound, was standing beside her and pulling her out of her chair. "How'd you do that? We're ten feet off the arena floor, at least. I swear there must be something in the water . . ."

"I choose—the Lady Lois!"

Thunderous applause.

She blinked. "What?"

"By the law of our land, the winner has chosen, and we are mated!"

Even more applause. My, my, the audience couldn't get enough of the old banging-hands routine.

"*What?*"

"All hail Princess Lois, she-who-will-be-queen!"

Pandemonium. Cheers. A few people jumped out of their seats, transformed in midair, and ran around the arena on all fours, yowling ecstatically.

"Ah, now you will be my daughter," the king said, sighing contentedly.

"Here comes that noise again," Maltese said, squinting wistfully up at her from the arena floor.

"*Aaaaaaagggggggggggghhhhhhhhhhhhhhhhhhhhhhhhhhh!*"

Chapter 7

"No."

"But it is the law."

"*No.*"

"But, my good princess . . ."

"Stop calling me that!"

They were in Damon's—*Damon's!*—bedroom. It was slightly smaller than the queen's, which was to say, the size of her apartment times two. He'd pulled her out of the arena, away from the rejoicing crowds, and now they had a modicum of privacy so she could rip him a new asshole.

"Lois, it is a great honor to be first chosen from the Bridefight, and—"

"How could you marry me without even asking?"

He didn't say anything.

"I didn't have a clue what today was about and you know it! It was a sneaky, nasty trick and you—"

"My princess shames me with her truthfulness."

"*I'm not finished,*" she snarled. They were nose to nose—well, her nose to his collarbone—and her fists were clenched at her sides. She kept them there. She was afraid if she didn't keep control of her hands, they'd load her gun and start pulling the trigger. The way she felt right now, that would be just fine. "You should be ashamed! I drop out of the sky yesterday, and today you fix it so we're married. *Married!* And if you think I'm gonna meekly trot off to your bed and be your princess and—and—"

"Give me heirs," he prompted helpfully.

"Damn right! Well, forget it. Y'know, where I come from—"

"You are there no longer."

"Shut up! I *know* that, you think I don't know that? Where I come from, the ladies get something called an engagement. For the benefit of the terminally stupid in this room, I will explain—"

"We also have a handfasting, but—"

"*I . . . will . . . explain.* An engagement is time to get used to the idea of getting married and, oh, I dunno, plan the wedding maybe? I mean, that was it? My wedding? You making a declaration in front of a bunch of strangers and we're hitched? That blows!"

She was doing fine, working herself up into a real fury, but everything rose up and hit her all at once, like a blow. She was married in a strange place, to a stranger who could turn into a puma, and one of these days she was gonna have to be queen. So if she stayed, she had to tolerate *that*, and if she went back home, what in the world—worlds—would she be returning to?

She burst into tears. Damon looked distinctly alarmed and raised his arms as if to hug her. She kicked out at him, nearly breaking her bare toe on his shin. "Get out," she sobbed. "Get out of here and leave me alone. I hate you."

He opened his mouth.

"Get *out!*"

He slowly turned on his heel and left. This was a perfect opportunity to do what she'd wanted to do for the last fifteen minutes, and she instantly took advantage of the situation. She threw herself on Damon's bed and kicked and yelled and cried.

"Lois?"

She rolled over and blinked up at the king. Her eyes felt swollen and sore. Her nose was stuffed shut.

The king was looking sorrowfully down at her. He had changed into fresh robes, and his hair was damp from the bathing room. She remained unmoved at his obvious attempt to make himself presentable before bugging her.

"We have wronged you, it is true. And now here is another truth—we do not wish it undone."

"This is how you cheer me up? Because you suck at it."

"Lois, we do not wish you to return. But you must also tell truths—do you honestly wish to go back? You are here because you lost something, yes? I can think of not one visitor from your world who wished to go back, in all the long years of my reign."

"Staying here's one thing," she grumped. "Being a princess and married without even being asked is something else." She pulled at the hem of her robe—God, there were yards of the stuff—and blew her nose on it.

"Do you not find my son pleasing?"

"Oh, he's gorgeous and you know it," she snapped. "And he's nice—when he's not tricking girls into marrying him— and a good fighter and he'll be a great king because he's smart and sneaky and everybody around here seems to love his ass, and he seems to like me all right, and he didn't eat me out in the desert when he had the chance, but still. He should have asked."

"It is not in the nature of a prince of the realm to ask," the king chided.

"Too fucking bad, Jack."

"My name is not Jack."

"Don't let the door hit you on the ass on the way out, *Jack*."

The king frowned down at her. "We have come to comfort you despite the many demands on our time, and now we are displeased," he said formally. "We require you to rise and adjust to your station and greet your mate, the high prince."

"'We' can take a long walk off a short pier. Buzz off."

He glared down at her. She glared back, and hiccuped. The corner of his mouth twitched—Damon's did that, too!—and then he said, "Perhaps for a bowl of *kumkoss?*"

"There isn't enough candy in the *world* to get me out of this bed. Now go away!"

"It is unseemly for a lady of your station to lie abed and sulk."

"I don't give a shit!"

"You will arise at once!"

"Wanna bet, fur face?"

He wheeled about and stomped out, looking like the world's oldest third-grader. She watched him go in gloating triumph. *Ha! Nothing's getting me out of this bed. I'm gonna lie here and sulk all damn week, if I want. Not budgin'* . . .

Damon poked his head through the doorway. "I will retire."

She sat bolt upright, and her complacency utterly vanished. *"Gaaaaah!* Don't you dare!"

"I only wished to come to my room for a brief rest. I had a tiring morning, in case you did not see." He was approaching the bed with an innocent look on his face, which instantly put her on her guard.

"Fine, I'll go back to my room. I mean the queen's room.

I mean . . ." She trailed off. Where the hell *was* she going to go? If she stayed in the castle, she had to sleep either in the dead queen's chambers, or with Damon here in his chambers, or . . . what? "Jeez," she said, "I wonder . . . maybe I should wish myself home and this whole thing will seem like a narcotic-induced dream. Maybe I—*mmph!*"

Damon had pounced on the bed, jumping a good eight feet across the room, and landed on top of her with one of his big hands clapped over her mouth. "Do not," he warned, his eyes two inches from her own. "Do not wish yourself away."

"Myyyyy uzzz ussss inking, ooooo oron!"

"Do you swear not to wish yourself away today?"

She glared at him over his fingers. *"Gnnnnggg nnggghh, ooo urg!"*

"Do you swear, Lois?"

"Mmph."

He removed his hand. She made a fist and thumped him in the middle of the forehead. "I was just thinking out loud, you moron. Don't pounce on me like a big cat. Even if you are one sometimes. I just about peed the bed."

"I apologize if you were startled. I did not wish to make you pee. I was unwilling to give you up so quickly." He shifted so he was lying beside her, propped on one elbow.

She rolled on her side so they were facing each other. "Look, what *is* it with you? And me? I'm a nobody." He opened his mouth. *"Don't* interrupt again! I'm not anybody important, and you're gonna be king someday. You could have anybody you wanted."

"That is true. And now I have."

"No, seriously."

"Yes, seriously."

"Damon! I mean it."

"As do I. Lois, did no one ever tell you? You are beautiful and courageous and wry and if those things were not enough for me—and they are, good lady—you bear the marks of a warrior."

"That's cellulite, Damon."

"You have fought battles."

"Battles with Ring Dings and Ho Ho's, yeah."

He ignored her lame-ass jokes. "You willingly place yourself in danger to help others. This is the true mark of a queen; this is why you were meant to be my mate. I—I did not ask you because it seemed obvious to me. To my family. And because once I found you, I did not wish to look for another. Nor did I wish to lose you to another. Did you not wonder why my good brothers and my father were also vying for your hand?"

"Oh, God, now you've given me a whole new thing to fret about." Against her will, she felt a warm glow at his words, which rang with sincerity. "You mean I could have been your stepmother?"

"No." This was said with such finality that she didn't crack a joke. "But we did feel it was fortuitous that you should arrive at such a time, during the Bridefight."

"Yeah, about that . . . you guys do that every so often, to pick wives? From princes on down? So it's like—like a Canis Royale? Except you're all cats. So what would that be? What's Latin for 'cat'? Felis Royale? Felix Royale? Shit. I took Spanish in high school, which isn't exactly helpful right now. Gato Royale?"

He waited until she was finished babbling, then said, "I do apologize, because I did you wrong. I thought—I thought you might be happy to be queen one day and if you were not happy . . . I hoped you would like me in time and be glad you stayed, and were my mate. I knew you had nowhere to stay, and thought you would wish to stay here. With me."

"I *did* like you, before you pulled this stunt, you big goober. Now I've got to wonder what else you have up your sleeve. When you bother to wear sleeves. Thanks for getting dressed before coming in, by the way."

"I did see you attempting to look everywhere but below our waists," he teased. "Are you never allowed to run free in your own land?"

"It's heavily discouraged," she said dryly. "And I've arrested my share of nudists. It's actually against our laws to be naked in public."

"It is breaking a *law?*" He gaped at her.

"Uh-huh."

"But what a good thing you are here now! You should not be forced to cover your skin if you do not wish it."

"It really hasn't been a problem before. Listen, Damon— now what? I mean, I can't stay here and be—you know. Married."

"Why?"

She sputtered. "Wh—because—we—well, we haven't even known each other two days, how about that?"

"This is not uncommon in my world—which is now your world," he pointed out.

She grunted and started to sit up, but he threw an arm across her middle and pulled her back down. She wriggled briefly, but it was like she was a tree trying to get free of the ground. "Oh, come on," she said, disgusted.

"Peace, Lois. I need rest, and I daresay you do, also. If you wish to leave in the morning, I will not stop you."

". . . really?" *Now, why was that so damned disappointing?*

"Really. But for now, rest. Perhaps things will seem less odd in the morning."

"Don't bet on it." But she let herself relax against him. She *was* tired. Exhausted, more likely. A shitload had happened in forty-eight hours. It was enough to make any girl's head spin. And she wasn't just any girl. She was the god-damned princess of the realm.

Even in her head, it sounded ridiculous.

The last thing she felt before she fell asleep was Damon's hands, gently stroking her back.

Chapter 8

She slept deeply, which was still a novelty to her. At home she'd slept poorly, if at all—her throbbing knee had killed her sleep and her dreams. But here there was no pain, and each night falling asleep was like sinking into a luxurious cloud. It was better than all the Ambiens in the world.

It was hard to worry about her problems—didn't take her long to get a whole new bunch of them, either—when she was so sinfully comfortable.

And she was *warm*, really very warm, but it felt wonderful, and smelled wonderful, and she stretched, luxuriating in the sweetness, and why was her blanket nuzzling her neck?

She opened her eyes. She couldn't see Damon's face, because it was pressed into her throat. He was kissing her throat and gently nibbling the flesh between her ear and shoulder. Goose bumps raced up her entire left side. She smacked his shoulder, which was not unlike smacking a cinder block.

"Rest!" she hollered at the ceiling. "You said *rest.*" There wasn't much light—so, the wee hours of the morning, then. Or the middle of the night. "Sneaky bastard."

He pulled back and looked at her. The light was poor, but she could see the gleam of his eyes, even in the near-dark. "Please," he said huskily. "Please, Lois."

"This isn't another trick, is it?" she said suspiciously. She was out of breath, which was irritating. "If we do the wild thing, it doesn't mean I'm fated to be the dowager queen or have kittens or something, does it?"

He blinked. "No."

"And it doesn't mean you're off the hook, right?"

"Off the—no, I don't believe so."

"Okay. Just so we're clear. This doesn't mean anything, and I'm still mad at you."

"Agreed."

"Okay. Then love me, you big idiot. Right now."

So he did. And she was lost.

He was hands and mouth and tongue and teeth, and big glorious dick. She hadn't seen one that size since—well, ever. Ropy with veins and throbbing against her hand and thrusting out at her from a nest of gingery pubic hair, she stroked it and played with it and marveled at it while he groaned against her neck. Then his mouth was on hers, his tongue was stroking her teeth, and his hands were rubbing up and down her body. It was relaxing and arousing at the same time.

"Ummm," she said into his mouth.

"Lois, you feel—you—oh, my good princess—"

She bit him. Unfortunately, he liked it. "Don't call me that, goob, you know I hate it."

He stopped licking her nipple long enough to look up and slyly ask, "Not even in the privacy of our own chambers?"

"*Your* own chambers."

"Ah, yes." He nibbled the flesh around her nipple, which made her want to scream, or bite, or something.

"Seriously," she gasped. "You're gonna wreck this by pissing me off."

"I would never dare anger my princess."

"*Daaaaaaaaaaa*-mon!" By now she was giggling too hard to sound impressively angry, and worse luck, he knew it, because he was doing plenty of laughing on his own. "You're a creep, an unrepentant asshole creep, and as soon as you make me come, I'm going to kick the shit out of you."

"Only a trueborn princess would dare talk to me in such a way," he whispered in her ear, and then nipped her earlobe.

"That's your explanation for everything," she griped, and reached down to tickle his balls. *That* stopped the teasing, she was happy to see.

He rolled her over onto her back and pushed her thighs apart. She squirmed against him, more than ready—*eager*—for what he had. He leaned down and licked her lower lip. "Now?"

"Yes."

Suddenly his fingers were between her legs, holding her apart, and she was reaching down to help him, and wriggling to meet him, and then he was filling her up, ah, God, he was so thick and so *long*, and warm, so deliciously warm, and what was he doing, coming inside her so slowly? Was he being paid by the hour?

She locked her legs around his waist and tightened her grip. Roughly, she grabbed his shoulders and yanked him down . . . and kissed him hard. "Are you going to do this in slow motion?" she growled, "or are you going to fuck me?"

"If I take your meaning correctly," he panted, and his voice was so thick she could barely understand him, "I will fuck you." Then he slammed into her the rest of the way, and a shriek of pure lustful joy gurgled out of her.

The giant bed was actually squeaking in time with their thrusts, and she hadn't thought anything could budge it.

She could feel his warm, firm chest pressed against her breasts, and she tightened her grip even more. She didn't ever want to let the big idiot go.

"Lois."

"Ah, God."

"Lois . . . this does not hurt?"

"No, and don't you dare stop."

"Not even if I wished, my good Lois. My own . . . Lois . . ."

"That's a . . . little better . . . than princess."

"My own Lois."

"Yes . . . like that."

She could feel his cock digging in and out of her, heard his harsh pants in her ear, felt his smooth muscles working toward their pleasure. His mouth found hers and she sucked his tongue into her mouth and felt him start in surprise . . . then eagerly deepen their kiss. His pure delight in their coupling tipped her over the edge; she clutched him around the waist as her orgasm bloomed through her like a dark flower. He was right behind her; his grip firmed until it was just short of pain, then she actually felt him spurt inside her.

They didn't move, or speak, for a minute or two. Just lay there, locked together, panting. Finally, Lois couldn't stand it anymore and broke the silence. "Holy shit."

"Is that good?"

"That's unbelievably, amazingly good. Um. Yum!" She tickled his ribs. "Rest up so we can go again."

He groaned and laughed in the same breath. "My Lois, you are insatiable."

"Actually, I'm frigid as hell, until I stumble across someone who knows what he's doing. And that was too sweet for a one-time-only thing."

"Ah. Then you will stay?"

She growled in response.

"For another day," he amended. "Stay through the next sunset, and then you can decide again."

A choice! Better yet, a way to save her pride. "Okay," she agreed. "One more day."

"Yes."

"Just one, though."

"Yes, my Lois."

"And your dad better not get his hopes up for grandchildren, either."

"No, my Lois."

"Because if we only do it three or four times in the next day or two—or three—the chances of my getting pregnant are pretty slim. Assuming we can even have kids. I mean, hello? Different species?"

He yawned. "Yes, my Lois."

"You think you've won, don't you?"

"Yes."

"We'll just see about that," she said. Then, "Is that you making that noise?"

"Yes."

"Well, jeez, how am I supposed to get to sleep with all that purring?"

"You will find a way, my princess—*oof!*"

"You're still in the doghouse, buster."

"I shall endeavor to get out, then."

She cuddled up to him. "As long as we've got all that straight."

"It is straight."

"All right then."

"I love you."

"Back atcha, you big jerk."

Several hours later, she stretched, rolled over, and opened her eyes. And yelped. Damon was propped up on one elbow, staring at her. "*Gaaaah!* Don't do that. Cripes, how long have you been watching me?"

"I do not know exactly. I was wakeful and it pleased me to look upon you."

She blinked at him. Her eyes had adjusted to the dark and she could see him perfectly well. "What time is it?"

"It will be sunrise soon." He bent to her and started nibbling the flesh between her neck and her shoulder. "And as long as you are awake, and I am awake . . ."

She chuckled. "You're insatiable."

"Indeed. Also," he added slyly, "it is my Bridenight. Such things are not uncommon on such a night, or so I am told."

"Don't start that again. As far as I'm concerned, this is just like any other night." *Any other night on a different world with a prince husband.* "Although . . ." She wriggled and rolled, and in a second she was straddling him. "I've had about enough of you taking the initiative, boy-o."

He looked vaguely alarmed. "What does that mean?"

"It means that this time, *I'm* in charge." She bent down and kissed him on the mouth, then the chin, then the throat. She stroked his nipples with her fingers and scratched lightly. He shifted beneath her and sighed.

"That is fine with me, Lois. If you get annoyed, you could bite me again," he added hopefully.

"Pervert." She licked his nipples and nuzzled the skin between them. She moved lower, kissing her way down his chest and stomach and thighs, until she was gripping his cock with one hand. She inhaled his musky male aroma, then leaned down and carefully sucked one of his balls into her mouth.

"*Loissssssssss,*" he groaned. "What are you doing?"

She was still holding his dick, which was throbbing

enthusiastically. She pulled back and licked the creamy drop off the tip. "What, you have to ask?" She licked the base of his dick, then slid her tongue all the way to the top, then down again, then up. Both his hands fisted in her hair; his breath came in ragged gasps. She straddled him again and guided him inside her. He seized her hips and thrust just as she came down to meet him.

"Oh, that's nice," she groaned at the ceiling as she began to ride him. "I can feel you in my throat."

"Lois . . ."

"Nice."

"Oh, my Lois." He pulled her down to him, kissed her hungrily, then caressed her breasts, drew her closer still, and sucked one of her nipples into his mouth. Meanwhile, she was still shifting her hips up and down to meet his thrusts, and when his tongue rasped across her nipple, she tipped over into orgasm. She cried out and rocked faster, then pulled back, seized him by the ears, and kissed him, shoving her tongue in his mouth, his luscious, hot mouth.

He sat up, pushed her back, and without breaking contact—without slowing their thrusts—suddenly she was flat on her back and he was surging between her thighs, working over her, sweat shining on his forehead as he pumped into her.

"Lois," he husked.

"Oh, God."

"Poor Lois, you will have to take me for some time. I am far from release."

She screamed as she came again, then locked her legs around his hips and thrust back at him. She was throbbing, and even though she'd come twice, she wanted more, had to have more. "Oh, God, Damon, that's so good. You're so big and it's so good."

"Because of you, Lois." He bent, kissed her softly, and when his fingers closed over her nipple and he pinched her lightly, she came again. "Only because of you."

She lost count of her orgasms. Everything was his cock and her cunt and their thrusts, his hands and mouth, the way he whispered in her ear and the smell of their sweat, their heat. Finally she was clawing at his back and begging him to come, almost sobbing, and then his eyes rolled back and he thrust once more, hard, and then he was spurting into her.

He collapsed beside her, breathing hard, and they lay like that for quite a while. Then he pulled back, kissed her softly, and cleaned her. Thoroughly. With his tongue.

She thought she was done, she thought it was impossible to have another orgasm, to wring another drop of pleasure from their time together, but when his tongue licked her out and swept over her clit, she thrust her hips toward his face and moaned at the ceiling.

He sighed and came up to her, and cuddled her into his arms. "Oh, my Lois. I love that sound you make."

"And I love your fucking *tongue.*" She kissed the hollow of his throat and breathed in his clean sweat. "God, Damon, you're really something."

"I am something," he said, stroking the curve of her hip and arranging the covers over them. "I am your mate."

She was too tired to protest and immediately dropped off into sleep.

Chapter 9

"**D**on't get your hopes up," she informed the king at lunch the next day. "I haven't decided yet if I'm staying."

The king frowned and opened his mouth.

"And *don't* give me any shit about it, either. Damon and I have come to an agreement, and I don't need you messing it up." The sternness of her statement was ruined when she pressed her palm to the king's forehead, checking for fever. "Are you sure you should be out of bed? You just got over being sick, then you had the Bridefight thing all morning yesterday—"

"I am well, Lois, do not fret."

But clearly he enjoyed her fretting. *This guy really needs a new wife*, she thought, feeling a stab of sympathy. She knew, too well, what it was like to be lonely.

"Did you and our son spend a comfortable night?" he went on innocently.

"Knock it off; you're about as subtle as a brick through a window."

"Then all that yowling we heard was merely—"

"Do *not* finish that sentence if you don't want my milk in your lap. If this is milk." It was milk colored, but thicker, and sweet—it tasted like a cross between coconuts and chocolate. She was on her fourth glass. *Damn*, the food here was fine!

Damon strolled in on all fours, in puma form. After giving her the fuck of a lifetime (again), he had bounded out of bed and left on a hunt with his brothers. Lois had briefly considered getting up, then sanity returned and she had gone back to sleep for five hours. "Morning," she said to him.

"Good morn, Lois. You are well rested and well fed?"

"Yes to both. Your dad's been getting on my nerves, though."

"I merely asked—"

"Don't try to defend yourself, Sekal," she snapped.

"Indeed," Damon said, shifting in a blink from puma to man. He thrust his arms into the robe Zeka was holding for him. "You do not wish to brave my Lois's wrath, my good father."

"No, indeed not," the king said with an admirably straight face. "What is this we hear about staying a day?"

Damon helped himself to a piece of bread from her plate. "She has decided to stay for the day. Tonight she will decide if she will stay for another day. We will 'play it by ear.' "

"I see."

"And if you don't like it, too damned bad," she said smugly. Sure, it was a sop to her pride, but that was all she cared about. Shit, for years, her pride was all she had. And the fact that Damon knew it, and respected it, had scored about a million points with her. "How 'bout that?"

"Hmph."

"Which reminds me," she said, staring at Damon's legs when he sat across from her, "I'll stay one more day."

"One more night, at the very least," Damon said, smirking.

Ooooh, if he wasn't so good in bed . . .

Before she could give him a piece of her mind, a commotion at the archway at the far end of the hall caught his attention. "Ah!" the king said. "Our visitors have come at last!"

"What's up?" she asked Damon.

"We have been awaiting these visitors from the far side of the SandLands. They wished to come for the Bridefight, but were too late, as you can see. We will clothe them and house them, and perhaps some will stay, and some will leave."

"Oh. Well, that's nice of you."

"Visitors are treasured, as you have observed. And we have heard that at least two of these visitors came to our world as you did, Lois. Such people are always interesting."

"Really?"

"Oh, yes. They tell the best stories. About auto-mobiles and gro-cery stores and the In-ter-net."

"And their Survivor game," the king added, rubbing his hands together, "with all the folk on an island and whoever stays last gets treasure."

"Yeah, American culture at its finest." Lois rolled her eyes, but stood to get a better look. There were a dozen of them, five men and seven women. They were wearing hooded robes the color of the sky. As they approached, they bowed deeply.

"Do not," the king said mildly. "You have come far and are weary. Rest here as long as you wish."

"Thank you, my good king. I am Themaya, and these are my companions. We regret our tardiness." As one, they all threw their hoods back.

Lois shot to her feet so fast, she knocked the table over. The one on the end—almost as tall as she, with that same dark curly hair, only hers was streaked with silver, and—and—

"Mom?"

Gladys Commoner stared up at her. "Lois? Oh my God, Lois, is it really you, baby?"

"But you're—"

Gladys simply stared, then held out her arms. Lois scrambled over the wreck of lunch and jumped down from the dais. In a moment she was in her mother's embrace. "Mom, I can't believe you're here, how can you be here?"

Gladys laughed, though tears were trickling slowly down her cheeks. "Honey, I don't have a clue. One minute I was driving to see your aunt, and the next I was in this weird desert with a purple sky, and Themaya and his band found me, and we've been traveling ever since. I've been here for ages and ages."

I thought it was suicides, but it must be anybody who's dreadfully unhappy. Unhappy at the exact right moment and the exact right time. Whatever it is, it's a fucking miracle.

"Mom, I can't believe it, I can't believe it. Oh, Mom, I missed you so much. When you—when you went away, everything went bad for me. Everything."

"Ah-*hem*." Lois and Gladys looked up. The king was looking down at them, hands clasped behind his back. His gaze was direct, but very friendly. He was staring at Gladys. "Are we to understand that this good lady is your dam? That Lois gets her good blood from this lady?"

"Uh—yeah, I guess. Mom, this is King Sekal. And this is my—well, my husband, I guess, Prince Damon. Damon, Sekal, this is my mom, Gladys Commoner."

"We are pleased," the king said, stepping down to greet her. "We are most pleased."

Her mother was staring at the king in a very unmomlike way. "I'm—it's nice to meet you, King Sekal."

"I am pleased, also, to meet my dam-by-mating." Damon bowed to her. "Your daughter is enchanting."

"Flatterer," Lois mumbled. Her head was still spinning. *Day three, and the hits just keep on coming.*

"And will you be staying long in our land?" the king was asking. He had taken Gladys's hand a few seconds ago, but hadn't let go yet. He was staring at her raptly. It was weird, yet adorable.

"I'd sure like to stay with my daughter, if that's all right, King Se—"

"Just Sekal, good lady." They stared at each other with identical goofy smiles on their faces.

Lois turned to Damon. "Okay, so, I'll stay the week. But no promises after that."

"No, no promises."

"Just the week is guaranteed, nothing else."

"No, nothing else."

"All right, then."

"I do love you, my Lois."

"I do love you, too, Damon. For the week, anyway."

They grinned at each other.

MATING SEASON

Prologue

She took her oath, and trembled with excitement and pride as she recited the sacred words. Her back was straight, heels together, chest out, the tip of her middle finger barely touching the outer edge of her right eyebrow.

It was too good to be true; it was a sweet dream from which she would rudely awaken. But for now, oh for now, she would enjoy it, and look to the future.

God help any man who woke her up.

Chapter 1

"Ah, but sweet and most helpful daughter of my heart—"

"Don't start that stuff again," the daughter of his heart warned him.

"Lois, surely you can tell me something."

The newest princess of the realm looked up from cleaning her Beretta and glared at the king. "Sekal, get it through your gigantic, thick head. I'm not helping you lay my mom, okay? I'm not giving you any sort of hint that's gonna help you hustle her into bed. I mean, you're a great guy and all but . . . yech. This is my *mom*, okay? Just . . . work it out on your own, okay?"

"But Lois . . ."

"La la la bah bah bah hmmm hmmm I'm not listening . . . la la . . ."

"Very well." The king stood up and started to stomp out in a huff. At the last moment he turned and said, "She *will* be mine," and then he was gone.

Lois rested her head on the tabletop. "Oh my God, I am so creeped out right now . . ."

"What is it, dear one?"

She perked up as Damon entered the room. "Your dad,

Damon. He's driving me most sincerely crazy. He's got the hots for my mom, how *weird* is that?"

"Not especially . . . weird. Your dam is very attractive for a woman of her advanced years."

"Not as advanced as you think; my dad knocked her up when she was fifteen."

"He *struck* his mate?" Damon looked horrified.

"No, no, it's slang for pregnant. She got pregnant with me when she was still a kid herself. But jeez, they've only been here . . . what? A month?"

"Your mother and her companions? One moonround, yes."

"And he's, like, all over her. It's weird."

"My mother was one much like yours, I think."

Lois had put her handgun back together and was now getting organized, but she looked up at that. "What? Your mom was from Jersey?"

"No, but she was not from our world. She just appeared one day, much like you did."

"And your dad met her and fell hard for her and that's why he's been alone so long," she mused aloud. "He's been waiting for someone closer to his own age, someone who comes from where we came from . . . hmm. That's very interesting, Damon."

"I know many interesting things," he said solemnly.

"Did she ever want to go back? Your mom?"

"No, I believe she was happy here. Although she did miss some things, as you miss the Dairy Queen."

"Don't say it. I've been dreaming of Dilly Bars. You guys need way more dairy products over here. Though I'm not sure a Blizzard would qualify . . ."

"My mother talked and talked about the Hitchcock when I was a child," Damon said. "Do you know the Hitchcock?"

"I've heard of him," Lois replied carefully. Ah-ha! Maltese! Her brother-in-law's funny name suddenly made sense. Damon was lucky he wasn't named Marnie. "Did she ever say how she came here?"

"Just that she was dreadfully unhappy where she was, and that her prayers were answered."

"Oh. I wonder what happens," she mused, "if someone *here* is unhappy. Do their prayers get answered? Anybody here ever just . . . pop out of sight?"

"To my knowledge, no. You might answer my prayers now," Damon suggested, smiling and holding out his hand.

Lois rolled her eyes. "You talk like you didn't just get some nooky two hours ago."

"An eternity of sunrounds," he said solemnly, then boomed laughter when she tickled his ribcage.

Chapter 2

Maltese, second in line to the throne, Prince of the SandLands, was, as the sister of his heart might say, bored out of his freakin' gourd.

"What *is* a gourd?" he mused aloud.

"What is a freakin'?" his youngest brother, Shakar, replied.

"Perhaps Lois will teach us her language."

"Or perhaps her mother will, 'less the king has her in his sheets already," Shakar said, and laughed.

"I do not think it will be as easy as you say. Look at our Lois. She was most unhappy to be made princess after the Bridefight . . ."

"For roughly one sunround," Shakar pointed out dryly. "Then our brother worked his customary magic, and now we have a new princess."

"Still," Maltese said stubbornly.

"I hope they—the travelers—choose to stay. Or at least, I hope Lois's dam chooses to stay. For Father's sake, if not Lois's. I wonder if her sire will pop up?"

"She did not miss her sire," Maltese said. "She *did* miss her dam."

"Do you think Lois wished for her, as she wished for her 'footlocker'?"

"I know little enough of such things, my brother. Only enough to know—"

"What a dullard you really are?" Shakar asked brightly.

"That one you will pay for," Maltese said, then pounced on his younger brother like a kitten looking for some fun. "Possibly many times will I require payment."

"Possibly many times will I thunk your—ouch!"

So they tussled and wrestled and bounced around the courtyard, but through it all Maltese had an odd feeling, as if this were some sort of play-act and not real. As if he were pretending to have fun with his young brother. Which was wrong . . . he *was* having fun . . . but always, always his mind was focused on the more pressing problem: Where was his mate? Why had she not arrived?

Worse: What if she never came for him?

Chapter 3

Best to stop fretting about it. Best to put his mind to other things, like being of service to his good king and he-who-would-someday-rule. Best to stop twitching and moaning like a kitten in heat and remember his responsibilities.

Faugh. Best to take a bath. Perhaps being clean would help his head—how did Lois put it?—"get clear."

He bumped into Sierr on the way to the bathing chambers, and she smiled at him but, at his request from many sunrounds back, did not lower to one knee or drop her gaze. "Good rising, my prince," she murmured, her sky-purple eyes tip-tilted and warm. "Require you some assistance this day?"

"No, Sierr. Be on your way."

"My prince," she said as he made his way past her. Though the hallway was more than wide enough to accommodate both of them, she brushed his shoulder as he passed and he smiled to himself. It would have been distracting and nice to have waterfun with the comely Sierr; she had rolled in his sheets before. But with his unruly thoughts all knotted up as they were today—as they had been for some time—he could not give her the attention she deserved.

Besides, she—she was not who he was looking for. He thought. He did not know *what* he was looking for. Or, for that matter, what he thought. Not for the first time, he envied Damon, whose charming princess had dropped almost literally into his lap.

In a rare show of events, he was the only one in the bathing chambers. Well, it was early, most people had work to be about. He did, too, i' truth be told. It wasn't worthy of him to sulk 'mongst the beriblooms and wish he were mated. He would wash quickly, and leave.

He stripped off his robe and stepped into the warm, fragrant water. He picked up a beribloom, crushed it in his fist, and began to work the lather across his shoulders and down his stomach. He heard a low sound, something like *thrumm-mmmmmmm*, and looked up, surprised.

He was even more surprised when the thrumming—a sound he had never before heard—got louder, and a bright gold circle of light suddenly appeared and spread wide, almost as wide as the bathing chamber. Maltese threw up a soapy forearm to shield his gaze, and as such almost missed the small form who fell through the circle of light and hit the water with a loud splash.

Just as suddenly, the noise cut off and the circle shrank down upon itself and disappeared with a whoosh. All that was left of recent events was the phantom circle imprinted on his eyes—it was everywhere he looked, and even now fading—and of course, the creature who had fallen through.

He waded to where it had fallen, stuck his arm into the water, and hauled it up as it sputtered and cursed.

Her. Hauled *her* up as she sputtered and cursed.

"Hello!" he cried joyfully. "I am Maltese." He hugged her to him. "I am so happy to see you!"

His response was a stinging slap on the side of his face.

Chapter 4

"Lieutenant Anne Sanger, Women's Army Corps, zero three three six two four eight nine one two." Ann smacked the guy again. He was so big, and so, er, hard, and weirdly slippery, that her slaps slid off him. "Lieutenant Anne Sanger, Women's Army Corps, zero three three six two four eight nine one two, *get your damn hands off me.*"

Obligingly, he dropped her. Instantly the water closed over her head, and she flailed about until she reached the surface. Her mind was trying to process too many things at once. The room, big and open and airy. The water, an odd color and an even odder smell . . . not bad, not remotely bad, but different. And the man. Big. Muscle-bound. Blond, with storm-gray eyes. And what was with that long hair? It was down to his shoulders, the color of gold and shadows, and weirdly, it didn't seem out of place. It should have; a man with hair like that would have had to fight out of any saloon he was dumb enough to walk into. But instead it went with the tanned skin and the big white flashing teeth and the intense gray eyes. It looked good. It looked *right.*

"Lieutenant Anne Sanger," she said again . . . she expected to say it many times, per her training. It had been one class out of many: What to Do If You Are Captured. Preceding it had been: How to Break Down an Army Carbine. "Women's Army Corps, zero three three six two four eight nine one two."

"That is very nice," he told her. "I am Maltese, second in line to the throne of the SandLands, Prince of the Exalted Ranges of the OnHigh Mountains, Lord of the Snowy Islands—"

"Are we in England?" she asked. It was one of the few places she knew of that had princes and lords. "How'd you do that? What am I doing here?"

"I wished for you," he told her, which was terrifying to the extreme, "and you came. You are here for me."

Chapter 5

"Damon! Lois!"

"Doors," Lois told her prince. "That's what this place needs. Fewer curtains. More doors."

She had just pulled the coverlet over herself when Maltese galloped in, wet and nude, pulling a young woman in an olive green uniform (also wet) behind him. She was frantically trying to free herself from his grasp, but since she came up to the middle of his chest, and his arms were as big around as her thighs, she was having no luck.

"Look! Look what is here!" Maltese thrust the wet woman at the startled couple on the bed.

"Lieutenant Anne Sanger," the wet woman told them. "Women's Army Corps, zero three three six two four eight nine one two."

"Nice to meet you," Lois said automatically. Damon jumped out of the bed (also nude) and bowed. The woman blushed harder, if that was possible.

"You're all in a lot of trouble," Lieutenant Anne Sanger continued. "Kidnapping a member of the Armed Forces—during wartime!—is punishable by—"

"How'd you do it?" Lois interrupted.

"Pardon, ma'am?"

"Kill yourself. How'd you do it? Welcome to the SandLands, by the way. You'll love it here."

"I doubt it," Lieutenant Sanger said. Her light blue eyes appeared to frost over as she continued, "I did not kill myself. I was getting ready to go on shift when all of a sudden I was wet. And here."

"I told you," Maltese said proudly, reaching for and attempting to hug her, and getting slapped back for his trouble. "I wished for you, and you came."

Lois was studying the woman. Really very cute, if you liked them small and dark-haired and fine-featured and blue-eyed. Which Maltese clearly did. The poor lug could hardly keep his eyes off her. Meanwhile, the lieutenant looked like she was ready to whip out a pistol and start busting kneecaps.

"What's with the uniform?" Lois finally asked. Then, "Damon, for God's sake, here's a sheet. Cover up. I *know*, don't give me that look, but the lieutenant is new here."

The woman mulled over the question, and just as Lois was getting ready to repeat it, louder, she replied, "I'm a WAC."

"A whack?" Maltese repeated.

Lois was so startled she dropped the sheet, then snatched it back up. "WAC? As in, World War Two babes in the Army?"

"I'm not a baby," the lieutenant said hotly.

"What—what year is it? For you, I mean."

Another odd look, followed by, "Nineteen forty-five. And I really, really have to get back to work. My country needs me. Please let me go."

"Oh, fuck," Lois said, and flopped back down on the bed.

Chapter 6

"But you can't keep her, Maltese," Lois protested. "She's not a stray dog, for the love of Christ."

"But she came here. Like you."

"*Not* like me. She's got a life she wants to get back to. She says she didn't kill herself. I think—I think maybe she stumbled across a—a thin space between our universes. Or something. And I guess those spots run through time as well as space . . . I mean, 1945? Jesus! It's 2010 where I come from. The war's—that war—has been over for . . . what? Sixty-five years? Where I'm from she's probably . . ."

Dead and gone, Lois had been about to say, but closed her mouth with a snap. Still, she got a sharp look from Damon, and imagined she'd be getting grilled later.

"Where is Lieutenant Anne right now?" King Sekal asked, the first time he had spoken during the hastily called meeting.

"In my quarters, of course," Maltese said. "Where else would I have put her?"

"She's not a mantelpiece, Maltese, you dumb-ass! You don't *put* her anywhere. Jesus, Jesus . . ." Lois rested her head on her hands.

"Maybe we should go talk to her," Gladys Commoner,

Lois's mother and the king's current hot monkey love interest, suggested. "Perhaps it will make her feel more at home
if she hears our stories."

"What, that we ended it all and woke up here? She didn't,
Mom, that's my point. She's here by accident. Not," she
said, glaring at Maltese, "because you wished for her. For
God's sake. She's a woman, not a Cracker Jack prize."

"I myself am not sure quite how it happened," Gladys
admitted.

"Good lady, we would hear your thoughts on this," the
king ordered.

Gladys colored slightly, but continued, "I just meant, I
don't know what happened. And Lois doesn't know, either.
I think what she said—thin spots between galaxies, or
whatever?—is as good a guess as any. Does anyone here
ever disappear?"

Damon, Maltese (Shakar was a-hunting, and wouldn't be
back for some time), and Sekal all looked at each other.
Then Damon shrugged the peculiar one-shouldered shrug
Lois had noticed of SandLands inhabitants. "Not that this
family has ever known. But the SandLands are large. Perhaps—"

"Well, that doesn't help us now," Lois interrupted. She
rapped her knuckles thoughtfully on the floor for a moment
(meetings were always held on floors, the attendees sitting
cross-legged in a circle), then said, "Well, I guess it wouldn't
hurt to talk to her. Poor kid must be massively confused."

"She will get used to the SandLands," Maltese said.
"And us. You did, Lois."

"Uh . . . I didn't have anywhere to go *but* here, Maltese. I
thought this place was the afterlife, at first. Shit, maybe it is,
I don't know. I studied criminal justice in college, not theol-
ogy."

"What is criminal justice?" Damon asked.

"What is afterlife?" Sekal asked.

"Later, you guys. Let's go talk to the lieutenant, first."

"Nice one, you goob," Lois said when they pushed the curtain aside and observed the palatial, yet empty, chambers that belonged to Maltese. She went to the window and far, far in the distance could see the tiny dot that was Lieutenant Anne Sanger, Women's Army Corps, zero three three six two four eight nine one two. "Jeez, lookit her go," she added, impressed.

"Where does she think she's going?" Gladys wondered aloud. "It's all sand out there. I know . . . I was out there for weeks and weeks with my group."

"I will bring her back," Maltese declared.

"Wait—" was all Lois got out before Maltese dived through the open window—from three stories up, the idiot!—transformed into a tan puma in midair, landed splayfooted in the courtyard, and bounded off after the lieutenant.

"Oh, yeah," Lois said. "This is gonna go *real* well."

Chapter 7

Anne had no idea where she was going, but staying put had not been, in her estimation, in her best interest. Fearless Americans did not sit quietly and wait to be tortured or brutalized or mocked!

Even better, the good-looking fool hadn't locked the door or the window. In fact, there *were* no doors or windows. But it had been child's play to climb down; she'd spent the first fifteen years of her life in Colorado and could climb before she could walk.

She ran, ignoring the stitch in her side, and kept her eyes on the odd horizon. Perhaps she could find someone sympathetic to the Allies. Perhaps she could find a gun. Perhaps she could wake up and find this was all a horrible, vivid—

She heard a thud-thud-thud behind her, methodic as a metronome, but didn't turn. In another few seconds, a large yellow cat was sprinting past her, then checked itself so hard it almost flipped over, then came to a dust-rising halt in front of her, which forced her to stop. In truth, she was glad . . . her side hurt like heck.

The cat looked her over then said, "Hello again. Need you a drink?"

No. He didn't *say* it. He thought it. At her. Because his

lips weren't moving, and even if they were, big cats—was it some kind of cougar? mountain lion?—didn't speak English. Didn't *talk*, for heaven's sake.

"It's bad enough you've kidnapped me," she said, staring furiously into the cat's storm-gray eyes. "But you get out of my head. Talk with your mouth, Charley."

At once, the large blond man was standing in front of her. Naked. Argh. "As you wish," he said cheerfully. "Are you ready to come back now, Loo?"

"Loo?"

"Loo-ten-unt. Loo," he added, "is the affectionate nick-name I have given you. My brother's mate has many nick-names for him. It is a sign of their joy with each other. Retard, idiot, dumb-ass, schmuck, loser . . . all these and more. What will you call me?" he asked, looking absurdly hopeful.

"How about Crazy Man?" She was trying not to look at his groin, and failing. She'd never seen a naked man in her life. His hair was much darker than the blond mass on his head. His penis looked long, but soft.

Stop looking at it, Anne.

She tried. And failed. In fact, she'd joined the WACs so she could see the world—and meet someone. But not like this!

"Are you not warm in those clothes?" He indicated her long sleeves, pants, and jump boots. Which, in the desert heat, were drying quickly.

She jerked back from his touch. "Don't even try to talk me into being a degenerate like you, you—you—you nudenik!"

"Ah, Nudenik! That will do. But Loo . . ." He took a step toward her, his long penis swinging against his thigh. She took a compensatory step back.

"You know what? Change back into the cat."

"As you wish." And boom, he was a cat again. It was the best trick she'd ever seen. If it was a trick. And of course it was. She was . . .

Dreaming. It was a dream! A very strange, realistic, odd, odd dream. She'd fallen asleep after a day of training and . . .

She pinched the skin on the back of her hand. It stung. She took a step toward the great cat, grimacing, expecting a bite, and touched the fur on the top of his head. Thick and plush, like an odd kind of silk, soft and warm under her hand. The cat cocked his head, but didn't bite or claw her.

She stepped back, thinking hard. The cat, thank the Lord, stayed out of her head so she could ponder. Okay, scratch dreaming. Ah-ha! She was being brainwashed! Someone had captured her and they were doing things to her mind. For what purpose, she did not know. She was a small cog in the great wheel that was the Women's Army Corps. But if she could just figure out how they were brainwashing her—

She covered her eyes with her hand and always, always, the great cat watched her, his eyes luminous with curiosity.

Nobody was brainwashing her. She wasn't dreaming and nobody was putting things in her head. She was not an imaginative girl, and she could never have thought all this up. And if she was being brainwashed, they wouldn't try to make her think she was in a strange place, with strange people who could turn into animals just by thinking about it.

She was here. It was real.

She burst into tears.

Chapter 8

"Now, my good lady . . ."

"Please, Sekal. Call me Gladys." The older woman smiled. "I've asked you many times."

"Yes, my . . . Gladys. Are your rooms comfortable? Are you finding our table with good things to eat? Because if not—"

"Sekal, my rooms are wonderful. Why, I had an entire apartment back home that you could have fit just into the room I'm sleeping in now. And the food is wonderful. To tell the truth, I don't recognize a lot of it, but it tastes delicious and it doesn't make me . . . I mean, my stomach doesn't . . ."

"She means, she's not getting Montezuma's revenge," Lois announced, walking into the great hall. "They're coming back, if you guys care."

"Who?" Sekal asked, gazing deeply into Gladys's brown eyes.

"Your second-born and the woman who dropped out of nowhere? Remember? Any of this ringing a bell? And if you inch any closer to my mother, Sekal, I'm shooting you in the face," she added irritably.

"Oh, now, you will not," Gladys said, jerking back. Sekal

had been kiss-close for a few seconds. She sighed. "I brought you up better than this, Lois. Behave yourself."

"Yeah, well . . ." Lois walked over to a window, pulled back the heavy tapestry in front of it, and peered out. "Dad canceled all that stuff out. That poor kid. She looks whipped."

"Exhausted," Gladys translated for Sekal, who looked alarmed. "Of course she does. Think how strange this place was to us, dear, and we came from modern-day Earth."

Lois watched the couple approach. Maltese was padding toward the palace in his puma form, and Lieutenant Anne was walking beside him, her head down, her arms folded across her chest. She looked desolate, to put it mildly. Maltese didn't look much happier.

"She got a room yet?" Lois asked without turning around.

"Yes, we have put her beside my Lady Gladys's room. I thought, the good lady being such a kind woman, she might help our visitor be settled."

"Oh, Sekal . . ." Gladys breathed. "You're so nice."

"Kindness to such a gentle lady is simple courtesy, my lady, and I would be kind to you, always."

"Oh, Sekal!"

"Barf," Lois said, still looking out the window.

"Ma'am, will you help me escape?" Anne asked dully.

The dark, curly-haired woman, who had been showing her where extra blankets were kept, slowly turned around. She was very pretty, about Anne's height, and was wearing a fern-colored robe. Anne was still in her uniform and, by the grace of God, would remain so. Those robes were more revealing than bathing costumes.

"I'm, um, not really the person to ask," the woman replied. She had a pleasing Midwestern accent, neither twangy nor drawly, and it comforted Anne to hear another American speak. About anything. "See, I'm what they call she-who-will-be-queen. Um, that means if the king—God forbid—dies, my husband and I are in charge."

Anne said nothing.

"So, um, I guess I could be considered one of *them*. Sorry."

"Dear, it's not that we don't want to help you." The older woman, Gladys, was still hard at work. She was an older version of Lois, slightly shorter and heavier, and had the same fox-like face and pretty eyes. She had bustled and fussed about the room, trying to make it perfect. It was a waste of time, in Anne's humble opinion, as the opulent rooms were as close to perfect as anything in creation. But it seemed to please Gladys to be busy, and so she rejected the first five coverings on the enormous bed, and was now smoothing out the sixth.

Now she turned to Anne, who was standing in the middle of the room feeling lost, and added, "We don't know how. We came here by accident ourselves. One minute we were driving, or . . . ." She shot a disapproving look at Lois. "Anyway, we don't know how we got here. We don't know how you got here. So we couldn't help you get back. We don't even know how to get ourselves back."

Her training prompted her to reply. "Thank you, ma'am."

"But this place grows on you," Lois said. "Seriously. I know that sounds like a load of shit . . . ."

Anne gasped.

Lois blinked. "What? They don't swear in 1945?"

"Women of loose . . . um . . . that is to say . . . ."

"Well, she *does* have a pottymouth," Gladys said primly, and Anne laughed for the first time that day. Both of the women stared at her, so she cut off the inappropriate noise.

"Ma'am, you were saying how this place, this strange awful horrible place that is not my home and will never be my home, you were saying, ma'am, that it grows on you."

"Uh, yeah. That's what I was saying." She and the older woman traded a look. "Don't you, uh, like Maltese? I mean, aren't you weirdly drawn to him? Even if you're pissed about being here? Aren't you thinking about him right now?"

As a matter of fact, Anne was. Specifically, she was thinking about that long soft penis, and what it might look like if he—if he liked her. She was wondering how that dark pubic hair might feel if her fingers were tangled in it, and she was wondering if she'd lost her mind at some point today. In fact, it seemed a certainty.

"Did you never want to escape, ma'am?"

The women traded another look. Finally, the crown princess—she-who-would-be-queen or whatever—sat down on the bed. "Okay, Anne. I'm gonna give you the straight poop."

"I appreciate that, ma'am."

"And stop calling me ma'am. I'm Lois, okay? Just Lois. And don't call me princess, or your highness, or anything goofy like that."

"Don't worry," Anne said dryly.

That made Lois laugh, for some reason. "Okay. Fair enough. Here's the thing. I wanted to be a cop—a police officer? For years and years."

Anne nodded. She could relate to that. She'd been born on a farm. Without the kindly intervention of World War II, she might have died on the farm.

"And I was, right? And I loved it. I never thought I'd love anything more."

"You were a police officer?"

"Yeah, I was a lieutenant in the—"

"In the offices, right?"

"No." Lois smiled. "I know what you must be thinking, but take my word for it . . . where we come from . . ." She indicated her mother with a nod. "Women can be cops, politicians, fly jets—"

"Jets?"

"—planes. They can do whatever the hell they want."

There was a long pause, and finally Anne said, "Ma'am, that is a lie. That is not true."

"Maybe in 1945, sunshine. But give it until the next century. I'm telling you, I carried a gun and I waved it at bad guys and got shot at and puked on *and* got paid for it."

Anne smiled; she couldn't help it. "That sounds wonderful."

"Excuse me," Gladys grumbled, fluffing up a pillow. "It certainly does *not.*"

"Where I am . . . I know it's wrong to be glad it's wartime, but my country needs me. Needs women. Because the men, God bless them, are getting killed. And finally we have our chance. We could get out of the kitchen. We could help. We could *fight.*" She looked around the gorgeous room. "And now I'm here. I—my country needs me. I can't stay."

Gladys opened her mouth, but Lois shook her head, and the older woman didn't say anything. Lois continued, "Look, I totally know how you feel. I couldn't see past my job, either, right? But then I got hurt. And they wouldn't let me on the street anymore. I could still be a cop, but I had to do paperwork and answer the phone . . . like that."

Anne shuddered.

"Right. And I put up with it. For a long time. And then I realized they would never, never let me do what I loved, ever again. And my parents were dead. I mean, my dad was dead. My mom was here. But I didn't know it. And I'd never been one to make friends, you know? So one night I killed myself. I took about a million pills and killed myself. Except I didn't die. I think." She turned to her mother. "*Are* we dead, do you think?"

Gladys shrugged.

"You weren't doing anything that would kill you when you came here, were you, Anne? I mean, you weren't charging a nest of machine guns or anything?"

"No. I was on my way to language lessons, at the base."

"Hmmm. Okay. Anyway. I woke up here. And Damon was waiting for me. And now I have a whole new life. A wonderful new life. All's I'm saying is, give it a chance. I mean, there must be a reason you're here. Even if you didn't do anything to get here. Right? Anne? Right? Mom, back me up here."

"I thought I was dead, too," Gladys said. "I was in a car accident . . . you know, a crash? And I woke up here. And my friends—the journeyers—found me. And I wandered around with them in the desert for a long time."

"Like Moses!" Lois said brightly, then ducked as her mother threw a pillow at her.

"At first I was shocked and unhappy, like you, dear. Then I got used to it. And then I met up with my daughter. And now I'm—well, now I have many friends, and the king has told me I can say as long as I wish, and my life is very different now, too."

Anne was listening, but she was more horrified than accepting. They wanted to be here? They never tried to go back? But that meant that she . . . that she . . .

"But there's nothing for me here," she said. She heard her voice tremble, and despised herself for it, but continued anyway. "Back home, they need me. Here I'm . . . what?"

Lois and Gladys looked at each other. "Well, there's no

war or anything. Which is a *good* thing. But, uh, Maltese really seems to like you."

"He doesn't know me. And I didn't leave the farm and join the Army so I could end up someone's wife somewhere *else.*"

Lois coughed. "Awkward," she said to the air. Then, "Right, well . . . um . . . anyway, maybe you could give Maltese a chance? To grow on you?"

"To *grow* on me? Like mold?"

"Okay, poor choice of words. Look, all's we're saying is, you're stuck here, right? Well, wherever you run to, you're still *here*. On this planet, or whatever it is. So why not stay in a comfortable palace with servants and a prince who really seems to like you, and just . . . give it a chance. Okay?"

"Okay," Anne lied.

Chapter 9

"Okay," Lois said, letting the curtain fall. She spotted Maltese lurking in the hallway, stomped over to him, put her hands on his broad chest, and pushed him back a few steps. "Uh-uh, Dr. Stud. You leave her alone."

"Is she all right? Does she still weep?"

"No, and no. Look, she's all tucked in and ready to go beddy-bye, so just, you know, give her some space."

His brow wrinkled. "Give her some space?"

"Look, I don't know if it's the dialect problem or if it's just that you're a guy, but back off of her, all right? Don't crowd? Get it? I mean, give the poor girl a break, she's kind of freaked right now."

"But I wish to be near her," Maltese said, sounding wounded.

"I *know*, Maltesc, believe me, I totally get it, okay? But she's not like me, she didn't—I mean, she's got stuff she'd like to get back to. She's really missing her life right now and she's mixed up, and doesn't have a clue what's going on. Just give her a chance to get settled in."

"As you wish, Lois."

"*Soooooo*. Turn around. Walk away."

After a minute's hesitation, he did.

Lois massaged her temples. "I had to end up on a planet that's never heard of Advil."

Maltese pulled himself up and swung a leg over the balcony, then landed lightly on the floor. He poked his head through the window, observed the lump asleep in the great bed, and sighed happily. Her scent was so pure, so delectable, almost like sweetmeats, and it was so strong it called to him. Why, his nose was telling him she was much closer than in the great bed, that's how strongly he was drawn to—

He heard a crash—inside his skull, oddly—and fell the rest of the way into the room.

"You get out!" he heard when he regained consciousness a few seconds later. "It's bad enough you've kidnapped me like the Lindbergh baby. But you're not going to sneak in here and rape me."

"Rape you?" he groaned, sitting up and rubbing the back of his head. "You mean wape? Prepare nuts and berries for you and anoint you with oils?"

"*No*, I don't mean *wape*. I mean—you know. When you have—uh—marital relations with someone who doesn't want to have marital relations with you."

Maltese frowned. "You mean, *force* you?" he asked, appalled. "Never! Not in a thousand sunrounds!"

"So why were you sneaking in my window? And where's your ladder?"

He did not know ladder, so he addressed the other question. "I wished to see you," he replied simply.

She flushed and brandished the other statue. He saw the room had at least six—perhaps not the wisest decorating move. "Well, don't do that! It's your fault I'm here. I don't have to like it—and I *don't* like it—but do *not* sneak into my

room and spy on me, or you'll get a lot worse than one of
these upside the head."

"I only wished to see you were all right."

"All *right?*" Her blue eyes bulged. "I am utterly not all
right! I have to get back to work, have you not heard me say
this before? There's a war, do you understand *war?* My
country needs me and I'm . . . I'm stuck in something out
of *Arabian Nights*. With people who can turn into leopards!"
She was wild-eyed and brandishing the statue, which Maltese
eyed with no small concern. "Isn't there someone in charge
I can talk to? Who can send me back?"

"My father is—"

"Never mind," she snapped, and glared.

"Perhaps . . ." he began, and hesitated. He did not want
her to go. But he felt her pain, keenly. Perhaps . . . perhaps
it was not meant to be? No matter how drawn he was to her?
The thought actually hurt him, as if someone had bitten
him in the stomach.

"Perhaps what?"

"Ah . . ." He rubbed his head again, but the swelling had
already vanished. "When Lois came here, she wished for
things. For one thing. Her footlocker. And it appeared. And
often, when people appear, they can wish themselves back.
As they can wish things from their world out of the air. So
perhaps . . ."

"You mean, like Dorothy in the *Wizard of Oz?*"

"I do not know Dorothy."

" 'There's no place like home'? Like that?"

"I do not know."

"Well, it's worth a try, right?" She set the statue down
with a thump, clasped her arms around herself, shut her
eyes, opened her mouth . . . then cracked one eye open and
looked at him. "Hey. Don't look so sad, uh, Maltese, is it?"

"I do not want you to go," he sighed.

She hesitated, then said, "I don't belong here. It's nothing, um, I mean, it's not personal . . ." He knew she was telling an untruth, that she held it very personal, but it did not seem courteous to correct her. "Well," she finished awkwardly, "thanks for the advice."

"You are welcome."

"Okay. Here we go." She closed her eyes, then opened them again. "Well, good-bye."

"Good-bye."

She closed her eyes again. Then she swore, "Cross of Christ!" And opened them, and hurried across the room, and stood on her toes, and kissed his chin. He blinked down at her, surprised, but before he could grab her and do some kissing of his own, she scurried back across the room and shut her eyes again.

"All right," she said. "This time I'm really doing it."

"Good-bye."

"I wish I was back at the base in New York," she said.

Maltese looked at the floor, imagining a gold circle would appear and whisk her away, as one had brought her, but nothing happened.

"*I wish I was back at the base in New York!*"

Nothing.

She opened her eyes again. "Maybe *you* have to do it," she said. "Because you—what did you call it? You wished me here." She gestured excitedly. "Sure, that's it! You have to wish me away!"

"But I do not wish for you to leave," he pointed out reasonably.

"Aw, shaddup! And wish me away already!"

"I wish Loo was back at the base in Noo Yorrrk," he said.

Nothing.

She stamped a small foot, and the hem of her robe flapped. "You have to *mean* it," she said.

"But I do not."

"*Arrrrggghhh!*" she screeched, and threw herself face-down on the bed. She kicked like a child for some time, then slumped against the bedcovers, exhausted.

He bent over the bed, and gently turned her over. "Are you well?" he asked with some concern. Her face was *very* red, and her eyes were leaking.

"No," she sobbed.

"Do you require anything?" This was, he felt, a foolish question—the one thing she wanted, he was unable to give her. Still, politeness had been drilled into him from his days as a tiny prince, and such habits were ingrained. "Shall I fetch Lois or Gladys?"

"*No.* Those two are useless to me. They *want* to be here."

"It is not such a bad place."

"Not the point. I finally had a purpose, I finally got out of the God-be-damned kitchen, and now I'm *here.*"

"Do not cry," he said, patting her ineffectually.

"I'm *not* crying," she sobbed. "And stop touching my head." She batted his hand away.

"Perhaps . . ." He trailed off. Again, an idea he wished he had not had. Again, he was powerless to deny her.

"What?"

"Well. My brother the good prince has shown me many times where Lois appeared. Lois thinks there are 'thin spots' between our worlds. Perhaps we could journey there tomorrow and perhaps your wish would work."

She stopped in mid-sniff and gaped at him. Then, slowly, "You'd do that?"

"I prefer not to. But I dislike seeing you weep."

She sat up excitedly, her head banging into his chin. "Really, you would? We could go there and try wishing again?"

"Yes."

She flung her arms around him and squeezed him with all her strength, which was puny, but he appreciated the gesture. He carefully squeezed back.

"I guess I misjudged you," she said, releasing him. "I really appreciate what you're trying to do."

"It is nothing."

"We'll see about that," she said, and grabbed the corner of his robe and wiped her face. Then she smiled up at him, and he saw that she had deep sweetmarks in the corners of her cheeks, what Lois called dimples. His heart nearly stopped, but he managed to smile back.

Chapter 10

"You're going where to do what?" Lois asked.

"The thin spot," Anne explained. "Where you came. Maltese is going to take me there, and wish me back."

"Wish you *back?*" The princess gave Anne a look that would melt iron. "What happened to giving it a chance here?"

"It was Maltese's idea," Anne said, feeling defensive and then feeling angry for feeling defensive.

"That is true," he agreed. "It was."

"Uh-huh. Well, good luck, I guess." Lois popped another white squashy thing into her mouth. It was the strangest breakfast Anne had ever seen, though she'd been too excited to try and eat. "Maybe I'll see you later."

"And maybe you won't," Anne said cheerfully. She wasn't going to let the prickly princess ruin her hopeful mood. Why, by twelve hundred she could be back on the base!

She followed Maltese out into some sort of courtyard, smoothing the collar of her uniform. She'd given in and slept in one of those robes, but had insisted on wearing her own clothes today. Thankfully, they had dried. Still, the robe had been comfortable, and sinfully soft . . . like silk. And a gorgeous wine red. Though it was early morning, the odd-looking sun was already high in the sky . . . another warm day. She could understand why everyone wore the robes.

Maltese stopped and was suddenly a mountain lion again, or whatever it was he could turn into . . . she had kept walking and nearly fell on him.

"If you would climb on, Loo," he said in her head—oh, she *hated* that—"we will get where we are going much faster."

She grabbed a handful of fur at his neck and carefully clambered onto his back. It wasn't much like riding a horse. Maltese was all funny bumps and odd angles. She gripped him with her knees and clutched double handfuls of fur. "You must be ready to be rid of me," she said through gritted teeth. How would she ever hold on while he moved? She could barely hold on and he was standing perfectly still.

"No," he said shortly, and moved off slowly, giving her time to adjust to his stride.

It was definitely an odd thing, riding a giant cat in a strange world on a journey where she would wish herself home. She supposed if she were a different sort of girl, she would be thrilled by the goings-on. Instead, they just made her more acutely aware of how different this world was, how much she wanted to get back home.

The funny thing was, "home" was the farm, and always had been. But she wouldn't have gone back *there* for all the tea in China. She supposed home was now the base. Though what she would do when the war was over, she didn't know.

She wasn't so foolish to believe, as some of the women did, that there would be a different place for them in the brave new world of post–World War II. "We have jobs now," they'd say in the factories, the show floors, the barracks. "We put down our spatulas and picked up our handguns and you can't go back, however the war turns out, you can't go back."

But you could. And they would. No, what would happen was simple: The men who had not been killed would come back. And they would want their jobs . . . every last one of them. So it would be back to the kitchen, back to the farm, back to the ironing board and the grocery lists.

Well, she would worry about that later. For now, she had to focus on *getting* back. Somehow.

"I'm not going to cry," she said. "I've done more crying in the last twenty-four hours than I have in the last twenty-four months, and I'm *not* going to cry."

"That may be so," Maltese said, "but your eyes are leaking."

"Never mind! Rats and double rats! You're not wishing hard enough, that's all there is to it."

"I have wished many times for you to go back."

"Something's not right. Because I'm still here, and we've been at this for hours."

Maltese shrugged from his cross-legged position on the ground. She paced angrily in front of him, occasionally kicking up a burst of sand and wishing it was going right into his face. She didn't quite dare do that, though she could fantasize, oh yes.

"Rats," she said again, and slumped to the ground next to him.

"It was worth trying," he said mildly.

"I haven't given up yet," she retorted, "and I'm not letting you give up, either. The cost of staying here is too high."

"The cost?"

"Right. For example. I just now realized you're naked. Again."

"Of course," he said, looking mystified.

"But that's the sort of thing I should have noticed earlier, don't you think? Where I'm from, you'd be in jail right this minute."

"Jail?"

"A cage."

Maltese shook his head. "Barbaric."

"No, civilized. Anyway, if I don't get back, who knows what other odd things are going to escape my notice? Hmm?"

He reached out and patted the top of her head, like a dog. "You could try it, if you wished. No one will put you in a jail if you decide to be sensible."

"Sensible?"

"It is a warm day," he pointed out. "You seem also warm."

She *was* sweating, but not so much because of the heat. It was him. Lounging around on the ground, casually nude, as if she was used to this sort of thing, as if she could control the urge to reach out and do some patting of her own. Which was ridiculous. Ridiculous! She had several dozen other problems to worry about; her new lack of self-control seemed the least of them.

"If I have to stay here for a while," she couldn't help asking, "can I stay in the castle?"

"Of course."

"That doesn't imply I'm giving up, you know."

"Of course."

"And I'd like my own room." She added, "Please."

"Of course."

"And don't read anything into this, either," she said, and leaned over to kiss him on the chin as she had the night before. Except he was too quick for her, seizing her firmly but gently, and she wasn't kissing his chin, but his mouth. He'd pulled her into his lap and something was digging into her bottom and she just knew what *that* was, and his mouth was on hers, and oh, he was warm and smelled like the sand all around them, clean and hot.

She put her hands on his chest and felt his nipple harden under her fingertips, and resisted the urge to rub it and see if she could make him as oddly out of control as she now felt, make him feel like nothing mattered at this moment except more touching, more kissing, more teeth and lips and tongue and—

She jerked herself out of his grip and he let her go, thank goodness (or was it, rats?). "That's enough of *that*," she wheezed, running her fingers through her hair in an attempt to look less mussed. Less kissed. Less curious about what else he would have done.

"As you wish," he said mildly enough, but his eyes were gleaming in a way that she wasn't sure she liked. The pupils were an odd shape, not quite long like a cat's, not quite round like hers. Egg-shaped? she wondered. Egg-shaped pupils? And when did I go crazy? Do they have nut hatches here?

"I think things are complicated enough without that," she said.

He said nothing.

"Well, they are," she continued. She realized she was still panting, damn the man, and fought to control her breathing. "For one thing—what's the matter?"

He was on his feet so suddenly she hadn't seen him move. He was looking out to the horizon and his lips were pressed so tightly together, they looked like a scar.

"Them," he said, almost spat.

"What is it? What's wrong?"

"There." He pointed. "The dark travelers. My father will not be pleased."

She looked, but all she could see was sand, sand, and more sand, stretching far into the horizon, stretching into the endless purple sky. She squinted until her eyes streamed, with no luck. But the effect on Maltese was shocking . . . he was like a different person, tense and stiff and glarey.

"What's a dark traveler?"

"Warmakers." He glanced over at her, seeming to remember she was there. "Come, Loo. We must get you back to the palace."

"But—"

"*Now.*"

He was suddenly the big cat again, and without another word she climbed on top of him. One thing she'd learned in basic training, if nothing else, was to obey an order. And Maltese, she realized anew, was a prince. He hadn't thrown his weight around once since she'd arrived . . . which made his tone all the more impressive.

No, annoying.

No, impressive.

Dammit.

Chapter 11

"We should have been more vigilant."

The castle, at first far off in the distance, was now rearing up in front of them; every thud of Maltese's paws brought it closer. She had been hanging on for dear life and wondering what a dark traveler was

(warmaker)

and if it was as bad

(warmaker)

as it sounded. Surely nothing could have been as bad as the Japanese, all those killer drones doing whatever their Emperor told them, why, it was indecent and . . . and un-American!

"I don't know," she shouted in his furry ear. "You spotted them right away. Before anybody. I couldn't even see them. I *still* can't see them."

"They crept up on us like scum," he continued, still sounding mightily mad.

"Scum?"

He put a picture in her head: a black sewer rat, its long, scabrous pink tail curled around it, its nose twitching, beady eyes gleaming.

"Oh, scum. Right. Maltese, you're being too hard on

yourself." *And you're running faster than I'm comfortable with, but never mind.* "The princess was telling me just last night that you guys don't have wars here or anything. If you're not used to it, you can't watch for it."

"We were easy," he persisted. "We have made it easy for them."

"We don't even know what they want. They have this thing where I'm from, the Welcome Wagon? Maybe they're bringing coupons and things. We don't *know.*"

"No one knows what they want. They don't speak; they grunt like animals." His loathing was rolling through her head, making her shudder. "They are animals, they come down from the mountains to make fights, they fight until the last scum-loving one is defeated, then they scuttle away."

"Okay, okay, I understand what you're saying, calm down, you're going to buck me off and trample me, and then how will I get home?" She tried to joke, to lighten his mood. "I see your plan now. It won't work."

"When we return, you must go with the princess and the Lady Gladys and the children, and you must stay with them until—"

"Wrong again, Maltese. Besides, do you really think *that* princess is going to cower in hiding with the babies?"

Silence, except for the thud-thud-thud of his paws hitting hard-packed sand.

"Right. And maybe I can help. I had a little bit of training before I ended up here. Maybe I can help you talk—"

"You do not go near them. You do not look at them, you do not touch them. You do not allow them to touch you. If one *does* touch you, I will eat his spine."

"It's good," she commented, "that we're establishing rules. For instance, being a newcomer here, I might not understand the whole 'don't touch or be devoured' guideline. And I've said this before—you're being too hard on yourself."

Silence.

"We have this place where I'm from," she continued doggedly. Her mouth was getting dry and she wanted a drink in the worst way. She blinked sun and sand out of her eyes and continued. "Pearl Harbor. It was the posting everybody wanted—the weather was kind of like here, breezy and warm but not too hot. And the ocean—that's like a big body of water—"

"We have seas."

"You understand, then. It was like paradise. You got to fight for your country *and* be stationed in Eden, what could be better? Anyway, my friend—my best friend from home—she was stationed there, and right before I signed up, I visited her at the base. It was like being in heaven. The palm trees and the—it was just really, really nice. And so I saw her, and she told me how great it all was, and it *looked* great, and I went away and signed up, and then the Japanese came and blew her up, and all her friends, too. And we never saw it coming."

"I am sorry for your friend."

"Yeah." She sighed. Her eyes were still watering, but she didn't think it was the sand. "Me, too. But my point is, I know what it's like to be asleep at the switch. You spend a lot of time blaming yourself. You feel so stupid, as if you were the one who failed. When the ones who deserve all the blame are the bad guys."

"So you especially want to go back," he said, slowing down as the castle gates came into view. "To avenge your friend."

"Well . . . yes."

"I see."

"It's just that I would feel better—"

"I understand, truly. I did not, before. I will not stand in your way again. When this . . . business . . . is taken care of, we will try again. And this time I will mean it when I wish for you to go away."

Stupid sand. She couldn't stop her eyes from tearing up no matter how hard she rubbed.

Chapter 12

"How long?" the king asked.

"Another sunround at most."

"How many?"

"Ten score."

"Excuse me," Princess Lois said, and thank goodness, because Anne had about a thousand questions herself. "I'm having some trouble with the whole 'sunround' thing. I mean, not that I should be focusing on that particular issue right this second, but honest to God, it's really been bugging me. At first I thought it was about a year, but sometimes it sounds like it's only a day. I know 'moonround' is a month, but—"

"It is easy to be confused," Prince Damon said, smiling at his wife. Anne privately thought that Maltese was just a tiny bit handsomer, but she was certain the crown prince could have crossed over to her world, gone to Hollywood, and made more money than Clark Gable. "A sunround is many, many sunrounds, as many sunrounds as it takes to get through Time of Sowing, Time of Growth, Time of Reaping, Time of Sleeping. But for the sun to climb into the sky and then fall down, that is just a sunround."

Anne looked at Lois, who was looking back at her. She almost smiled at the totally confused look on the princess's face. "What?" she asked.

Lois cleared her throat. "So what you're saying, sir, is that a sunround is a year, but a sunround is a day?"

"Yes," the king, the crown prince, and Maltese all said in unison.

"You *got* that?" Lois exclaimed.

"Please, we must keep our attention on the dark travelers," the king said, an almost absent reprimand. "If they are coming, it cannot bode well."

"It hasn't before?" Lois asked. "I thought you guys didn't have wars."

"There are occasional . . . skirmishes? Small fights?"

"Great."

"What do they want?" Anne asked. "Where I'm from, the fight is for more territory—"

"I read somewhere that all fights are actually land wars," Lois commented. "That no matter what the politicians said it was about, it was actually land spats. Revolutionary, Civil, World War One, World War Two, Korea, Vietnam, Gulf . . ."

"Oh my God," Anne said, revolted. "There are more wars after Pearl Harbor?"

"Well . . ."

"It does not matter what they want," the king said, again guiding them back to the subject at hand. "They must be stopped, and driven off."

"Okay, uh, that's not too open-minded," Lois said. "Will it hurt to hear them out?"

"They don't speak. They're animals," Damon explained. "They come and try to make war, we defeat them, they leave. A few sunrounds later, they try again."

"I assume you mean years and not days," she muttered.

"And that's an interesting perspective, calling the dark travelers animals," Anne commented, a little startled at the sudden, surprising burst of prejudice in what had seemed to be a friendly and welcoming people. Certainly they had made Gladys and Lois welcome, as well as Anne herself. "You know, since you all . . . um . . ."

"I don't think you should go there," Lois suggested.

Anne wasn't sure what that meant, but she persisted. "Since you can all turn into animals. It seems, uh, odd, that you would call strangers animals and fight them off. And then tell visitors you don't have wars."

"You are new here," the king said, courteously but firmly. "You do not understand our ways."

"We have learned in the past they do not understand us. They do not speak as we do; they care only to take what is not theirs."

"Is that not what war is like at your home?" Maltese asked her.

"No, no. See, the Nazis invaded and then the Japanese joined up and they're . . . you know, they're hurting people and they hurt a whole bunch of us because they don't want to lose the—well, it's a totally different thing."

"Nazis suck," Lois agreed. "Don't sweat it, Anne. History backs you up."

But she was troubled. The Japanese were wrong; the Germans were wrong. And Maltese's reaction to the dark travelers was also wrong, very very wrong. But, er, how, exactly? And what could she do about it?

"So what's the plan?" Lois asked, and again, Anne gave silent thanks. The outspoken princess was, as usual, collecting information she herself was after.

"You and Gladys and Loo and the little ones will—"

"—get our guns and help you guys go kick some ass," Lois finished.

Anne laughed aloud at the look on Damon's face, then clapped a hand over her mouth as everyone looked at her.

"Except my mom doesn't have a gun," the princess continued thoughtfully. "Not to mention the kids, obviously. I can lend Mom one from my footlocker, but she won't use it."

"Why not send a party out to meet them?" Anne suggested. "Perhaps we can find out what they want."

The men shook their heads, and Lois rolled her eyes at Anne.

"At the least, they'll know you're ready for them," she persisted. "You might be able to run them off without anybody getting hurt or bombed. I mean killed."

"It is not the way we deal with them," the king said.

"Well, I'm not hiding while you go out and fight, pal, so just forget about it," Lois informed the prince.

"What does it cost to try?" Anne persisted. "Lois could stay here and supervise while you send a small party out to talk to them. If things go badly, you've got time to get back here and prepare."

"Who says the dark travelers can't beat them back? I wouldn't want to be in a footrace with any of them. I mean, no offense, fellas, but it sounds like these guys just wander around the desert all the time. They must be incredibly tough."

"They're only half men," the king sniffed.

"Animals," Damon added.

"You mean . . . they *can't* change into the big cats like you boys do?" Anne asked, suddenly understanding.

"*That's* your problem with them? But we can't change, either," Lois said.

"Yes, but you cannot help it. You were born on another star. You have overcome your difficulties admirably. You don't skulk and sneak and steal land."

"Oh, is that the difference?" Lois replied, but it was clear from her expression she didn't understand at all.

Chapter 13

"That was very sneaky," Anne told Maltese as they neared the dark travelers.

"I cannot help it if I think you are wise, Loo."

She grinned, and since she was on his back again, he couldn't see her. To her secret amazement, she and the princes and the king were riding back out to where Maltese had seen the travelers. Lois was marshaling the troops, the women, and the children back at the palace. Anne had never considered that for a moment, but instead persuaded Maltese to let her meet with the travelers. Well . . . bargained.

"Just so we understand, I'm only staying until Time of Reaping," she reminded him. "Less than half a sunround."

"Yes, I understand."

And in return, the king allowed the unthinkable—for a stranger, a protected female, to meet the scum. Er, dark travelers.

It wasn't that they didn't think women could fight, Anne realized, wishing once again she had a drink. It was beyond foolish; she was running around in the desert (well, *she* wasn't, exactly) without a canteen. And no one had suggested one, which told her they simply weren't as susceptible to the heat and the sand as she was.

No, they thought women could fight just fine . . . in itself a novel experience. In fact, these people *valued* women who could fight—women like Lois. But the princes had to weigh that value against protecting future queens and princesses. And, she thought with a secret smile, Damon was so ridiculously protective of Lois, it was adorable and sort of funny at the same time, because Lois just would not stand for it, not for a moment.

Maltese, however, was a much more practical fellow. And they had quickly struck a bargain. She couldn't let such an opportunity go by, and if it meant lingering in the Sand-Lands a bit longer than planned, well, she'd face the consequences of that later.

"I do not like this, my good son," the king said in her head. Yech! Both for talking in her brain, and the sentiment.

"My good king, are you not tired of it always being the same with the dark travelers?" Maltese replied. "It costs nothing to give Loo her chance."

"I dislike change," the king replied, "but perhaps the perspective of a newcomer will be helpful. And I would wish to put an end to the difficulties between you and your visitor."

In other words, Anne thought, *the old guy wants his son to settle down. And I guess I'm in line for the job. Because I fell into the pool when Maltese wished for me! Ridiculous.*

Still, it was nice to be included. She was riding Maltese, as usual, while Damon and the king ran along either side of them, *sans* riders. The other prince, whose name she'd unfortunately forgotten, had gone hunting a few days ago and would not return in time.

If it was me, I'd be mad, she thought, momentarily sorry for the absent prince.

But it's not me, she thought, and was for a moment joyously, deliriously happy. She felt like she was starting an adventure, like the first day of Basic, like the day she'd left home. As for the possible danger, she knew to her bones Maltese wouldn't let anything happen to her. That feeling was very strange, but also comforting.

She slid off Maltese's back and watched the dark travelers approach. They didn't look terribly frightening. In fact, they looked dusty and hot and tired, like regular people at the end of a particularly long day in the fields, not the lowlife boogeymen the royal family had made them out to be.

Their robes were long and black (in the desert? she thought incredulously) and flapped in the wind. Their large hoods were off and hung down almost to their waists. And they were all brunettes, their hair varying lengths and shades of brown.

The royal family, Anne realized with a burst of excitement, were all blond. In fact, except for Lois and Gladys and Anne herself, everyone was blond. It was a country of Betty Grables and Errol Flynns! (Er, wait, wasn't Flynn a brunette? Oh, never mind.) Yes, a country of blonds . . . except for the dark travelers, of course. But this wasn't really their land, was it? No brunettes allowed.

They looked human, too, she realized as the man in front opened his mouth to speak. *If I was riding the bus on the base and these fellas got on, I wouldn't give any of them a second look.*

She supposed that was part of the problem. In a land of godlike creatures, the dark travelers had committed the sin of being ordinary.

"*Glzpllk sltsl dkst,*" the man in front said, and he interspersed the small pause between consonant clusters with a glottal click.

"I'm sorry, we don't understand you," Anne said, hoping he would reply.

"*Sltsl gdpsll wjjkswwkkt?*"

"It's gibberish," the king sniffed. "In a moment they will begin to quarrel and fight us."

"It's not gibberish," she corrected him, almost sharply. "It sounds harsh to our ears because they don't use vowels."

"*Sltsl gdpsll wjjkswwkkt?*"

"Do . . . not . . . fight . . . else . . . shalt . . . be . . . defeated," the king said slowly and loudly.

"*Sltsl . . . gdpsll . . . wjjkswwkkt?*"

"DO . . . NOT . . . FIGHT! ELSE . . . SHALT . . . BE . . . DEFEATED!"

"SLTSL . . . GDSPLL . . . WJJKSWWKKT!"

"Okay, that's enough of that right now," Anne said. "For heaven's sake. It doesn't matter how loud you are, or how slow, if neither of you understands a word."

"We did warn you," Damon said mildly.

She ignored that. "It's obviously a standard greeting; note how they're repeating the same consonant set. It's not gibberish, it's definitely a language." She clicked her tongue at the man in the lead, and though he did not smile, the frown wrinkles in his forehead smoothed out. "It'll be hard to learn . . . God, it'll be hard! Worse than Mandarin. But I think it can be done."

"How . . . how do you know these things?" Maltese asked in amazement.

"I'm studying dialects at the base," she replied. "I was supposed to be sent overseas to—well, we were still working on that while I was in training." At their looks of confusion (the ones who *didn't* speak her language seemed to be

following it better), she elaborated. "I'm . . . when you sign
up to fight, you have to take a lot of tests, and all my tests
showed that I have a knack for languages . . . do you know
'knack'? Yes? One time we had a guy from Paris—I mean
he was originally from Paris, but he'd been living in
America for years and years—he was on the farm for a couple of months helping my dad with the spring planting, and
he taught me French. I was pretty fluent in time for the
Fourth of July picnic."

"Are you telling us you can speak their tongue?"

"Give me a couple of months first."

Maltese smiled at her, and she couldn't help smiling
back. When he looked at her like that, his whole face lit up
and it was nearly impossible to resist.

"You are wonderful," he said.

Chapter 14

"Sir, I'll have to meet with them daily. And I'll need lots of paper and pencils—you have writing materials? Frequent, short sessions or we'll all burn out. And I'll need an assistant, someone to bounce ideas off of and help me get it all down. Can we barrack them close by?"

"It will all be as you wish, Anne," the king assured her. "But I must warn you, the minute they turn warlike, they will be dealt with."

"Sir, be serious. They're just happy to be included. Look at them."

The dark travelers were following behind the four of them, and Anne kept glancing back to make sure they were still there. None of them had smiled yet, but they had chattered excitedly to each other and followed her willingly enough.

"And they will be guarded," Sekal added.

"I understand, but please try not to be too obvious, all right? They haven't done anything wrong. And *we* invited them back to our home." She corrected herself. "Your home."

"Because of you," Maltese reminded her.

No, she thought. *Because your father loves you and wants you to be happy, so he's going along with this in order to make me happy and therefore you happy. So now a pack of dark travelers are staying in the palace for the first time in the history of Sekal's reign. Because of me. So I'd damned well better learn that language in the next five months.*

Or else . . . what?

Chapter 15

"You mean there wasn't a fight? You brought 'em back here and we're having a slumber party or whatever? Well, shit, that's great!" Lois did something to her handgun, and the clip slid out and slapped into her palm. They didn't have guns like that in the service, so small and sleek and black, and Anne was longing to get a closer look at it. Well, maybe when she knew Lois better. "I can't believe it! Where's Damon, I gotta go give him a big hug."

"They're getting the dark tra—" Anne shook her head. Part of the problem was that ridiculous name. "They're making our guests comfortable. I guess the king didn't want to leave it to the servants."

"Huh. Okay. So, what were they like?"

"Mild and unwarlike," she replied. "I think they're just tired. They've probably been roaming the desert for decades."

"Like Moses," Lois said brightly.

"Stop saying that, it's annoying. Maybe they got tired of it and a new leader tried to take things by force once or twice. It would never work, of course, so they were stuck being nomads. You should have seen them when we motioned for them to come with us. They were so surprised.

And grateful. Now I've just got to learn the language and we can really make some progress."

"Wait, wait, I missed a memo or something. You're *staying?* To learn their language? Cripes, I miss out on one afternoon jaunt and everything changes."

"I have to. The king needs me." She heard herself saying that and straightened with pride. *The king needs me.* Oh, boy, did that feel good. Not "ride your bike to the vet and tell him the cow's having trouble bulling" good. "Report to Special Language and Tactics at 0800" good. "It's no wonder everyone here thought they were animals."

"Yeah, I have to admit, it's the first evidence of prejudice I've seen," Lois said. "I was kind of shocked. I guess I've only noticed Damon's good side. I mean, once I got over being massively pissed at him. He's so gonzo, I guess I overlooked that prejudice."

Anne guessed what "gonzo" meant based on context. "Yes, he certainly is. Well, everybody has hidden dark corners, I guess. Otherwise there would never be wars."

"That might be oversimplifying a little, doncha think? I mean, there's gotta be more to it than—"

"Speaking of wars," she continued, "did I hear you say a while back that we won World War Two?"

"Yup. We completely kicked their asses. But later we made nice with Japan, you know, after massively obliterating them, and now we—"

"We made friends with them?" Anne was shocked, thinking of the dead at Pearl Harbor. "After what they did?"

"Well, uh, we sort of got even with a vengeance. Do you know what Fat Man and Little Boy are?"

"I guess the important thing is we won," Anne said, not really listening. "I'll be sorry I couldn't do my part, but maybe after I learn the language of the dar—of our guests, I can work on a way to go b—"

"Oh, for Christ's sake!"

"Where I'm from," Anne said evenly, "ladies don't speak in such a way."

"Well, wake up and smell the fucking roses, sunshine. You *aren't* where you're from. You're here. You were bitching and moaning because you finally had a purpose back home and got taken away from it. Well, shit! You've got a purpose here, too, one a lot more important than being a cog in the war machine back home, I might add. You *stopped* a war, for crying out loud!"

"A skirmish," Anne couldn't help correcting.

"And now it turns out you're this humongous language expert and we're massively dependent on you to talk to them, and you practically negotiated a peace treaty just by talking the king into giving them a chance, and who knows where this is gonna lead, but *ohhhhhh noooooo*, poor Lieutenant Anne, trapped in the SandLands with no purpose." Lois's voice was dripping scorn, and Anne squashed the urge to smack the princess between the eyes. "Don't you get it? People don't end up here by accident. This was meant to be! Will you quit crying about it and accept your destiny already? All this bitching about not being in training is getting *real* old. Will you just please suck it up?"

"Excuse me, Princess," Anne replied, her scorn equal to Lois's. "I've been here, at my count, less than seventy-two hours. I beg your pardon for not acclimating quicker. How dare you lecture me, *Princess?* You have no idea of the realities of being a woman in 1945. You weren't even born while I was struggling to make something of my life. How can you know what it's like?"

"I ought to by now," Lois snapped back, "after all the whining I've had to put up with."

"Then you've got an idea how trapped a person can feel, a person with few choices and fewer opportunities. Then you get a chance . . . and you're free. But not for long."

"No, then you get a new job, a very important job, and a prince thinks you walk on water and does everything he can to make you feel better, plus, hello, could he be more great looking?"

"What does *that* have to do with anything?"

"But *noooo*, that's not good enough for you, *you* have to get back to the precious base—"

"I would think," Anne said quietly, "that as someone who killed herself rather than face life without her job, you might be a little more understanding. I can't do mine and you have the *gall* to tell me to 'suck it up,' whatever the hell that means? How did you do it, Lois? Did you shoot yourself with that nifty little gun? Did you jump off a building? However you did it, you most certainly did not *suck it up*."

That got her, Anne saw at once. Lois's mouth had dropped open but she made no response, because there was none.

"So in the future," Anne finished, "if you would keep your unsolicited opinions to yourself, I would be grateful." She turned and left the small sitting room, passing a slack-jawed Damon on the way out. Lois was right about one thing at least: this place absolutely needed doors. "Don't say a damned word," she told him. "Dammit!"

Maybe ladies didn't use vulgar language, but it was an interesting (and refreshing!) way to express oneself, for certain.

Chapter 16

Maltese had brought her lots of thick paper, so heavy it was almost like cloth, and pots of a thick, viscous substance which looked like tar but wrote like ink, and shiny sticks to dip into the pots. She tried to make notes about the afternoon, but the argument with Lois kept breaking her concentration.

True, the woman had overstepped her bounds, princess or not, but she had certainly given Anne something to think about. Was there meaning to all of this? She had almost convinced herself ending up in that sweet-smelling pool had been an accident, a divine joke, but now she was wondering. Because she certainly had a job here, had purpose, and couldn't—wouldn't—leave until their guests had secured a place on the planet. It was as much their home as the royal family's—but persuading Sekal of that might take some doing. She would stay until it was done.

As for the war back home, she already knew how it ended. And she sincerely doubted that the contributions of Lieutenant Anne Sanger would have much of an effect on the outcome. Certainly the farm didn't need her—her father had replaced her with a hired hand the week she had taken the oath. And her mother, of course, had escaped into death years ago.

She stuck the stick into the pot, determined to make a record of the day's progress, no matter wh—

"Is there still danger, Loo?"

She looked up. Maltese had pulled the heavy curtain aside and was standing in the doorway.

"Pardon?"

"I was only wondering if it was dangerous to speak to you." He grinned. "Certainly Lois thinks so."

"Oh, her." Anne put the stick down on a different sheet of paper, mindful of the stains. "She picked a fight and I decided not to roll over, that's all."

He made a noncommittal noise and approached her. "What is it you are doing?"

"Making notes about today. Trying anyway." She stared at her hands for a moment, then looked up into his beautiful face. Of course, his looks were irrelevant. But they certainly didn't hurt matters. "Maltese, do you think all this was meant to be? That I was supposed to come here?"

He knelt beside her chair then picked up one of her hands, turned it over, and kissed the palm. "Loo, I thought that before you helped us make a home for the lost ones."

"The what?"

"It is a small improvement over dark travelers," he said, "and the king has bent an attentive ear to you in this matter, as in many others." Smiling: "I think he has too much fear not to obey you."

"Oh. You're right, that *is* better." She was mildly amazed that her smallest suggestions were being taken so seriously—definitely a novel experience. "So that's what you think? That I'm supposed to be here?"

He paused, as if he were trying to find a way to speak his mind without scaring her, and finally said, "I think if it was not meant to be, you never would have come. And if your coming was a mistake, you would have been able to go back."

She looked at him steadily, this good man, this prince, who had never bossed her and had never made her feel rotten for being born a girl. "Can I stay here?"

"Of course."

"With you?"

"Of course."

"Forever?"

He kissed her for a lovely long time. "Of course."

Chapter 17

Lois pressed her lips together so tightly they went white, then turned and glared at Damon when he prodded her.

"I guess maybe I was out of line," she said to Anne, still staring daggers at Damon.

"And."

"And I shouldn't have given you all that shit."

"And."

"And it wasn't for me to tell you to suck it up."

"And."

"And I'd better not push my fucking luck unless I want to sleep on the couch for the rest of the week."

"What is a couch?" Maltese asked.

"It is a thing where you cannot mate," Damon explained. "It is a terrible, terrible place."

"I appreciate that," Anne said quickly, biting her tongue so she wouldn't laugh. Lois looked so annoyed; Damon, so earnest. "I said some things, too. Things I regret." Not the whole truth, but her brand-new sister-in-law was obviously trying to make up for bad behavior; it wouldn't hurt to meet her halfway.

At least, she *thought* Lois was her new sister-in-law. Or sibling-by-mating, as Maltese called it. There hadn't been a priest, or even a justice of the peace. Instead, the king had pronounced them mated, then gone looking for Gladys. It was a bewildering, abrupt end to a dizzying week.

And she didn't regret it in the least. The moment she had stopped fighting her destiny, as Lois had called it, a feeling of incredible goodwill—dare she call it inner peace, if there was such a thing?—had come over her. Suddenly the SandLands had seemed especially beautiful, the people around her especially kind, the castle especially opulent. And to think it was now partly hers! As a member of the royal family, she was entitled to a share of . . . well, everything.

And she knew exactly what she would do with her newfound influence. What she had been doing all week . . . being an advocate for the lost ones. She doubted it would be her life's work—she had many helpers willing to learn the language as quickly as she could translate it, and two years from now, communication should be reasonably simple. But there would be other things to occupy her time. Her duties as a princess royal, and perhaps later . . . children.

Odd, how something she had never given much thought to was now on her mind all the time. Well. Not children, exactly. But the making of them. Which, judging from the way Maltese had been looking at her all evening, would commence as soon as they had some privacy.

"I have to tell you something," she said nervously. They were alone, finally, sitting on Maltese's silk-covered plain of a bed, and he was kissing her between her neck and shoulder, causing delicious shivers to race up and down her spine. "I should have told you earlier. But in my defense, there wasn't time."

"I did not wish to give you time," he whispered, nibbling

on her ear. "I feared you would change your mind and run away with a lost one."

She couldn't help but laugh. "That was pretty unlikely." She leaned away from him. "I'm serious, I have something important to tell you."

"Can you tell me from beneath the bedclothes?"

"No." She slapped his hands away. "Listen, I'm happy to be here and I think we'll have a wonderful life together, but I have to tell you, this isn't my first time."

"First time? Yes, you're new here."

"No, I mean I'm not a virgin."

His brow furrowed. "You mean . . . you have mated before?"

"Not been married before, but I've—you know. You remember the man who taught me French that spring? Well . . ." She paused. "I was curious. And that accent was really wonderful."

"Loo, I do not care."

"Well, you say that now, but I know men usually do care about that sort of thing. And I didn't want to have this discussion after and have you think you were tricked. It's silly, but—"

"Loo. I do not care even a small amount."

"Really?"

"*I* have mated before," he pointed out.

"Well, yes, that's usually how it is. Uh. I mean, that's how it is back home."

"This is your home now."

She smiled at him. "So it is. Kiss me some more. Your reaction was quite a bit nicer than I thought it would be."

He obliged, his tongue exploring her mouth, and soon enough she had wriggled out of her mating robe and helped him out of his, and she was kissing him all over his broad chest and he was sighing and stroking her hair.

"You really don't care?" she asked again, because she was having a little trouble believing it was this easy.

"Loo, I beg of you, can we please talk of something else? Or better, not talk at all?"

"All right, all right. Let's talk about how beautiful you are."

He laughed and caressed her bare hip. "Men do not have beauty. You are the beautiful one."

"Pretty is as pretty does . . . not that I ever knew what that meant. And I'm supposed to be a linguist."

"You will teach me the tongues you speak?"

"You want to learn Spanish? Or Mandarin?"

"I have interest in what interests you."

"Oh." She reached out and tentatively grasped him, marveling at the way he throbbed in her hand. He groaned a little and shifted so she could have better access. "*Te quiero.* That means I want you." It also meant I love you, but she wasn't quite ready for that yet.

He breathlessly repeated the phrase, then reached out and stroked the fine hair between her thighs. His finger slipped through her wetness and he gently caressed her, his thumb lightly pressing her clitoris. She felt a little breathless herself, and felt herself yearning toward him as he eased her legs apart and his other hand joined the first, stroking and teasing.

She let her head fall back and gloried in his hands, his tongue in her mouth, his lips on her throat. When he held her apart with his thumbs, she strained to meet him, nearly sobbing as his hot length slipped into her, as easy and pretty as a dance.

She clutched his broad shoulders as he surged against her, as he pulled her thighs up so her legs were wrapped around him, as he stroked so hard, and yet so sweetly, she nearly felt it in her chest. In fact, she did feel it in her chest; her heart was filling, bursting.

"*Te gusto,*" she moaned, and meant it the way it was supposed to be.

"Say a truth," he murmured to her.

"I want you."

"Say another truth."

"I . . . love you."

"I, also."

"Please don't stop."

"Never."

She had meant touching her, filling her up, but realized he had meant he would never stop loving her, and then she did weep, a little. But it didn't feel like being weak, being a silly girl; in this one moment between them, it felt exactly right.

She felt a flower full of light open inside her and shivered as she reached orgasm, shivered and tightened her grip, and then he was stiffening in her arms and telling her that he loved her in Spanish.

After, they cuddled together in his big bed, his hand cupped loosely over her right breast, her head on his shoulder. "It's nice to be home," she said after a long, comfortable silence.

"It was not home for me until you came," he replied. "I have waited for you long and long."

"I guess I was waiting for you, too. I just didn't know."

"But now you do?"

"Yes." She sighed. "Now I know."

They slept.

He woke before she did, and she supposed she would get used to being gazed upon while she slept. On the other hand, she wondered, is that something one would ever want to get used to? She never wanted to take any of this— or him—for granted.

Although she had been here just a short time, it felt like she had been fighting forever. Now that she had stopped, she wanted to preserve the feeling of sublime contentment.

"How dull," she commented, "that I've turned out to be like all the other girls, interested only in home and a family."

"I do not think you are dull, Loo. And I do not think your interests lie only with heirs."

She reached down, found him. Quite hard for her. The thought—the clear proof of his wanting—brought a warm flush to her body.

"It doesn't sound like you think so," she teased.

"Mmmm . . ."

"Show me what you like. Do you like this?" She slid her palm up and down, her thumb and forefinger meeting at this tip, then spreading apart at his base.

"Oh *yesssss* . . ." he groaned.

"What else? We're married now, I'm supposed to know these things." She heard her solemn, almost scholarly tone and smiled. "So tell me."

"Touch . . . my gems . . . in your other hand . . . while you do that . . . that . . ."

She cupped his testicles, marveling at their furry warmth, their pleasing texture, while her other hand stroked up and down. (And it seemed, whatever the planet, men had valuable names for their testicles, something she would think about later, when it would be more appropriate to laugh.) He was squirming beneath her touch, his hands gripping her shoulders, and then he wrenched her down for a toe-tingling kiss.

In half a second, he had shifted so that he was leaning

over her, his hands were busy below her waist, his fingers making her squirm, making her groan, making her want him more than she had ever wanted anything. His fingers stroked and dipped and teased and she writhed beneath his touch, pinned to the bed by his kiss, his hands, her desire.

He eased into her, never breaking the kiss, and she rose to meet him, looped her arms around his neck, and met every thrust. She felt his hands cupping her bottom and sighed into his mouth. Then he was stiffening over her and looking chagrined.

"I was too soon," he said. "I apologize."

She laughed out loud. "You've got the whole rest of your life to make it up to me."

"Agreed," he said. "I will start at once."

And he was as good as his word.

GROOMFIGHT

Chapter 1

Prince Shakar was the queen's own child, which was why he missed all the excitement. Unlike his brothers, Shakar could not get enough of his mother's world, and the only way to get there from the SandLands was through stories.

As a child he had heard about The Hitchcock, The Chubby Checker, Chocolate Sodas, the Dirty Stinking Commies, and the king of the land, Eisenhower. When Princess Lois came, she regaled him with tales of Those Bastards in Payroll and the World Wide Web, marvelous updates to a world he had come to love as much as his own.

In short, because Shakar was his mother's son, he spent quite a bit of his time wishing he was somewhere else.

Thus, hunting trips. He could never get to his mother's world by hunting, of course, but it helped to get out of Castle Royale for a few sunrounds.

In fact, if he had not been his mother's son, he would not have missed the dark travelers and Anne's great cleverness, her mating ceremony, his trip, the farm, the Groomfight, and Rica.

He owed his mother everything.

Chapter 2

He had almost caught up with the herd of toans, and sup-posed it was time for the kill. Although he doubted he would, in fact, cull; his father had taught him never to kill unless he was hungry. He was tracking the toans to keep in practice, and out of boredom.

He sniffed some offal, judging it to be from just that morn, and thought, *How I wish I were anywhere, anywhere but here*, and then fell.

This was startling, to put it mildly, and he instinctively shifted back to his two-legged form. He had fallen, some-how, *through* the sand, and was surrounded by golden light, so bright it made his eyes water, and he fell and fell, and thought, *See now, you have your wish and are you not sorry?*

He landed with a tooth-rattling thud and knew no more.

He awoke and found himself looking up into a glorious face, a smiling *kumkoss*-colored beauty with the biggest, darkest eyes he had ever seen.

"Well hiya," she said. "Are you okay?"

"Yes," he replied, dazzled.

"Are you sure? That was quite a fall. From the sky, if you don't mind my pointing that out."

"I am well."

"Glad to hear it, bud! You think you can sit up?"

"No." It occurred to him that his head was pillowed on her soft sweet lap, and he had no urge to move. Ever.

"Okay, take your time, get your wind back." She brushed his hair out of his eyes, her full bosom actually blocking the sun for a moment. "I haveta say, you gave me quite a shock! Not to mention you almost landed on me."

"I ask forgiveness."

"Don't worry about it," she said cheerfully. "I have quick reflexes. And it livened up what was looking to be a dull morning. D'you want something cool to drink?"

He could have thirsted on her, gazed upon her forever, but after watching his brother woo Lois, knew better than to blurt out such a thing. Although it was the tradition to explain openly about feelings the moment they were discovered, it tended to startle Earthers.

"I am fine." And he was. Her oval face was framed by wings of dark hair streaked with silver, and she had a small nose and chin, and the proud cheekbones of a queen. Her voice was low, almost throaty, and her fingers as she stroked his forehead were cool.

"I'm Frederica Callanbra, but you can call me Rica."

"I am Shakar, Prince of the S—"

"The SandLands, right?"

"How did you know that?" he asked, so startled he sat up.

She was kneeling beside him, and he saw she was wearing short clamdiggers, only to her knees, a plain sky-colored work shirt, and nothing on her feet, which were dirty. It was quite a bit cooler there than his home, he noticed, and there were a great many trees, casting shade over them. He could smell domestic animals and vegetation. Quite a bit of it, more than he had ever smelled in one place at once.

Never mind sky-colored shirt, he thought, glancing up. *The sky here is a different color. How beautiful it is!*

"My mother told me about the SandLands," she explained, smoothing an errant strand of dark hair behind her ear.

"My mother told me about here," he said excitedly. "About clamdiggers and sodas and all the many costumes you all wear. She came from here."

"Well, my mom came from *there.*" They sat in the dirt and smiled at each other. "Prince, eh? You're a long way from home."

"I am glad to be here," he said with perfect truth. In addition to trees as tall as the castle, there was a lush green covering on the ground. "My mother was a good queen and a good mate but she did miss her home. She told me about grass and oak trees and . . . farms?"

She gave him an odd look. "I work the land, sure. But I'm here by myself. If you're looking for a settlement, the nearest one is a day's ride from here."

"I am not looking for a settlement."

"You seem to be feeling better. Want to come in for something to drink?"

"Yes, I would like that."

"Nice and easy," she replied, extending a hand to help him up, not that he needed assistance. And not that he was about to refuse her touch. "You okay? You feel dizzy or anything?"

He did not know "dizzy" but forgot about it as he stood to his full height . . . and realized she was as tall as he was. Such a thing had never happened to him before. The tallest woman at the palace had come up to his throat. "You are large," he replied, very surprised, then flushed as blood surged to his face. Fool! A terrible thing to say to a female. "I meant to say, you are very big. Ah . . ."

She laughed. And did not seem offended! "My dad was even bigger . . . a whole head taller than me. My mom was the shrimp in the family. And may I say, that's quite a way with words you've got there."

He laughed, too, relieved and a little surprised at how quickly she put him at ease. Rica was quite a woman.

Chapter 3

"This is very good," he said, draining his third cup. "What is it?"

"It's just milk from the animals. You probably saw them outside."

"And you are here all alone?"

"Yeppers. There was a—a plague, I guess you'd call it, and my folks got exposed when they were getting supplies. We called it the Five-Minute Flu, because you had about five minutes to make your peace and then you choked to death on your own snot." Rica said this to the amazing stranger with perfect calm, though ten years later, the memory still hurt. No chance to say good-bye; the last thing she'd said to her mother had been, "Don't forget to bring back sugar."

"By the time I came after them to see what was holding them up, everybody who was gonna catch it had caught it, and . . . well. I figure being a hybrid helped me fight off the disease. I've never been sick a day in my life." She sighed. "Poor Mama and Dad."

The prince blinked at her. She had time to marvel at his eyes—she had never seen eyes the color of grass before—when he asked, "You have stayed out here alone?"

"Well, there's work to be done. What was I going to do, abandon the family home to . . . what? Go find strangers? And eventually, the town settled again. We're like the *old* Colonists, you know, the ones who came to America? We get the shit kicked out of us, but we always bounce back. Besides," she added matter-of-factly, "where was I going to go? I didn't have any—I mean, like I said, there's always work to be done."

"You remind me a bit of my sibling-by-mating, Lois. She also is from here and—and is brave with her words."

Rica laughed. She'd never heard it put so tactfully before. "Yeah, brave with my words, yeppers, that's me. So, listen, how are we going to get you back?"

"Back?"

"Well, sure. Did a—I don't know, a spell or something— did that go wrong back home? Or do you have machines that toss people all over the galaxy and one of those went wrong? How'd you end up here?"

"I do not know," Prince Shakar replied. He didn't look even a tiny bit troubled. "What matters is that I am here now."

"*Ooooookay.*"

"I must earn my keep," he told her earnestly. "I cannot lounge about your family home eating and drinking. I must help you."

"Oh, uh, that's not really—I mean, you're a prince. You—"

"—must not let others take all the work on their own shoulders," he finished firmly.

"Well . . ." She was weakening. Although he was fascinating to look at and talk to—she hadn't seen skin that color since her mother died—there was always work to be done. And he looked strong. A little on the small side, but strong. "I guess there are a few things . . . if you don't mind . . ."

He set his cup down with a decisive thump. "I do not mind. Please show me what is to be done."

"If this was an eighties movie," she said, grinning, "there'd be a musical montage of us working together and bonding right about now."

"Beg pardon, what?"

"Never mind. Let's go, Prince."

"Shakar."

"Prince Shakar."

"No, only Shakar."

"Gotcha."

"You are *strong,*" she commented several hours later. "I've never seen anyone pick up a full-grown barnyard animal before. I thought I was in pretty good shape, but you . . ."

"It seemed the best way to get her into the barren so she could be with her young one."

"Barn."

"Yes." He looked her over and she almost blushed—the expression in his eyes was admiring and even a little—"You are strong also. Many of our females are strong, but I do not know if they could tend to a holding this size on their own. Lois is not strong at all," he added thoughtfully, "but her courage makes up for it."

She shut the gate and bound it closed with the thick rope. No roaming animals tonight, thank goodness! "Yeah, I know how that goes . . . my mom was much stronger than my dad. It didn't bother him, though. They used to tease each other about it. She'd pretend that the way to decide who would get a chore would be to arm wrestle, and of course she would always win, and—"

"Arm wrestle?"

"Yeppers, it's when you—uh, here." She stepped closer to the gate. "Here. Put your arm up like this . . . yeah, rest your elbow on the top . . . okay, and then I do like this . . . and now we—*owwwwwwwwwww, stop* squeezing! That's not how you do this."

"I apologize," he said, his tanned face coloring to his eyebrows.

She pulled her hand out of his grip and inspected the mashed fingers. "Okay, new rule, no more asking guys who fell out of the sky to arm wrestle. Lucky for you I'm—what do you call it—I can use both hands just as well."

"Why would you not?" he asked.

"Oh, I guess everybody from the SandLands is—ambidextrous! Got it. I was afraid it would be on the tip of my tongue all day."

"You had fear it would *what?*"

"Never mind. Yeah, come to think of it, my mom could use either hand . . ." She shook herself. "Okay, back to business. Now *carefully* wrap your fingers around mine . . . yes, like that . . . and now we each try to push the other person's arm over. *Get* that other hand *down*, not like that, that's cheating."

"Many apologies." He was inspecting their joined hands with interest. "Now what do we do?"

"Okay, now . . . go!"

She strained and even grunted, and to her surprise his arm actually went over a couple of centimeters, when she realized . . .

"How long should the game last?"

"Oh, for the love of . . . will you just push my arm over already? Ow!" She glared while he looked guilty. "Fine, great, good work. Give me my hand back, I want to make sure I still have five fingers."

He didn't give her her hand back. If anything, his grip tightened. "I should not play that game again," he told her soberly. "I would never want to cause harm to your hand or—or any other place."

Uh? "Uh . . . that's okay, Shakar. It was just for fun." He looked so earnest, so sweet, so sexily sweaty (it had been a long afternoon), she couldn't think of what to say. Was this real? Sure, she was a homesteader, a colonist, and she was used to odd things happening, but they were usually *bad* odd things. Not godlike gorgeous fellow dropping from the sky and being sweet and helpful things.

"You know what?" she said at last, because he was entirely too close . . . kissing close, if that didn't sound too absurd. "You want to cool off?"

He blinked. "Cool off?"

Chapter 4

"This . . . is . . . *wonderful!*" he bellowed as he launched himself from the old rope and landed with an enormous splash in the middle of the largest outdoor bathing area he had ever seen.

She laughed as he paddled around her like a puppy, and splashed him when he got too near. "Told you. This is just the thing after working on the place all day."

"The water is so odd . . . it smells different."

"Well, I guess. You're not in Kansas anymore, Dorothy."

"No, and I suppose the Lion and the Scarecrow are lingering nearby as well."

"I hope not. How'd you know—oh, your mama told you."

"She told me many things." He dived under the cool water, which smelled a great deal like the grass, peeped at her bare legs, then resurfaced. "She also mentioned Negroes. I think that is fascinating. Everyone has the same-colored skin at home. It is quite dull."

"Oh, is *that* what she mentioned." Rica laughed again. Shakar loved the sound. It was like the gurgling of a child, innocent and sweet. "And catch up, fool, it's not Negroes.

And it's not African-Americans anymore, either. It's colonists. Small *c*."

"Small *c*-letter," he repeated obediently. "I do not understand why others of your kind were cruel because your skin was darker. I would like to have skin the color of a kumkoss," he added wistfully. "It would make hunting much easier."

"No it wouldn't." She shook her head, and water droplets flew from her hair. "Your skin is the color of the sand back home, right? You're perfectly evolved to hunt there. But as to understanding the whole issue . . . you got a year or two for me to explain it to you?"

"A year?"

"Sunround," she corrected herself.

"Oh, yes! I have many of those."

She gave him another odd look. "Well, I was only kidding. That shit was a long time ago, excuse my language, and it doesn't really matter anymore. We've been in the majority for a long time."

"So have I," he said cheerfully.

"I'll bet, Prince."

"Thus, we are perfectly . . ." Mated, he had been about to say, but was wary of frightening her. " . . . suited," he adjusted.

"Think so, *Prince?*"

He splashed her, and her laughter changed to choking. She suddenly disappeared and, while he blinked water out of his eyes, felt a tug on his leg and then he was the one gurgling and coughing out odd-tasting water.

"You are sly," he told her when she resurfaced.

"Keep it in mind, Prince. Don't spit, that's nasty."

"I do apologize. The water is different."

"Different, yuck, or different, hmmm?"

"It does not taste bad," he assured her, "just different."

"Oh. Well, I love this little man-made lake. It's always so refreshing. I look forward to jumping in all day."

"Do you bathe here?"

"No, there's a head back at the house, with soap and everything. I just come out here to get cool."

"At home—"

"You've got those big bathing pools inside, right? Do you even have lakes or ponds?"

He thought and thought, and finally said, "Just the sea. There is the sand, only the sand, and then suddenly there is the sea. Only the sea."

"*Ooooooooookay.* Sounds like a dream vacation spot."

"I will never see it again," he said, dismissing his birth planet with a wave of his hand. "It does not matter. It is lakes and ponds I must get used to, and soap and heads."

"And Negroes," she added dryly. "Don't forget those."

"Colonists with a small *c*-letter," he said obediently.

She had been swimming away, shaking her head, but at that she abruptly turned and swam back to his side. They treaded water, facing each other.

"Wait a minute, you're serious? What are you talking about, never see it again? How come? Did they send you away? I can't imagine you did something *that* bad."

"No, I was not sent away. I wished to come here. I have always wished to come here. And finally, my wish was granted. It happens at home, only the other way . . . people from your world fall into ours. Except not only the other way," he added, correcting himself, "because your dam came *here*."

"Well, yeah. It's kind of funny, it was exactly like this— Dad was working on the farm, and Mom fell out of no place and landed right in the pile of ma—never mind, the point is, she was surprised to be here, but she never . . ." Rica trailed off, troubled. "She never wanted to go back," she finished.

"That is how it is." Still, his heart cramped at the thought of never seeing his good father or brothers again, or Lois, or the small ones she would bear Damon.

"Well, it doesn't have to be."

"Yes," he assured her, "it does."

"Does not! I mean, just because my mama never wanted to go back doesn't mean she couldn't. Dad built her the machine and everything."

"What?" And again, "What?"

"Hello, how do you think we got here? He was an engineer way back in the day, and after she told him about the SandLands, he went into town, talked to the Elder, brought back part of the machine, modified it, and Mama could go back home whenever she wanted. Theoretically, I mean. She never wanted to go." Rica thought about that a moment. "I think that's part of the reason Mama settled in so well. Part of the reason Dad built the thing in the first place. She knew she could have gone back anytime, and that made her never want to go back. I bet he was counting on that. He was a smart guy, my dad."

"Your father was a—a builder?"

"An engineer, yeah."

"And he made a MASH-een that could send someone to the SandLands?"

"Muh-SHEEN, and yeah, he did."

Shakar was gaping at her. She could practically count all his teeth. "When you were alone all this time, why did you never go visit the home of your dam?"

Rica shrugged. "I don't know. Mama never wanted to go back. So I couldn't think of a good enough reason to leave here and go someplace that Mom disliked so much, she never looked back."

"Buh—wh—b—"

"Maybe you should get out of the water and lie down," she said, concerned. "You look kind of weird."

He had swum to her and was holding on to her shoulders. "You have never used it? Not even to settle your mind? Never put it in motion even if you yourself did not journey?"

"No, I—oh, I get where you're going. No, I didn't push any buttons for fun. Whatever's making people pop out of nowhere, it's not Dad's machine. Maybe it's a residual effect," she added thoughtfully. "Something about the traveling . . . the ships . . . maybe it tore a—a thin spot or whatever between our planets. Making it easier to go back and forth—or maybe someone, somewhere, built the same thing my dad did, and he or she *is* pushing buttons for fun. Also, your fingers are digging into my shoulders."

"Forgive." He abruptly released her. "I was just . . . taken by surprise. I did not realize . . ." He trailed off. "I did not realize . . ."

"But that's good news, Shakar. You can go home whenever you want. Probably. I mean, nobody's tested it, but my dad knew his shit. And I've maintained the machine; he did it every week, and after he died, I made damn sure I did it every week."

"You know this machine?"

"I know all the machines on this place. It's the advantage of being a single girl." She smiled.

"I guess . . . you are correct. It is good news. I had thought . . ."

"Well, do you want to go back right now? We can dry off and I'll show you where I keep—"

"No," he said, seeming to come to a sudden decision. "I do not want to go back right now." Then he gripped her shoulders again, pulled her to him, and kissed her wet mouth.

"I knew skinny-dipping was going to get me into trouble," she murmured, looping her arms around his neck and kissing him back.

Chapter 5

She had wrapped her legs around his waist, hoping they wouldn't drown (but such a way to go!), and Shakar supported them easily in the cool water. Consumed with curiosity, she reached down and found him, hot and pressing against her palm and like rough silk in the water.

"Not to kill the mood or anything," she said, nibbling on his throat, "but my parents died when I was fourteen."

"I am very sorry," he replied, cupping her bottom.

"Thanks, but what I meant was, I've never done this before."

"No?"

"I've been really busy the last ten years," she said defensively. "I never quite got around to going to town to lose my virginity. To buy feed, sure. But not the other. Anyway, my point is, if you don't want to do this—"

"No."

"—too damned bad. I've waited long enough." She paused and realized what he'd said. "Oh, no? Good. I mean . . . let's just say, I'm a big believer in signs, and when a great-looking guy falls out of the sky and is nice and gorgeous and sweet and great-looking, I'm gonna jump him."

"As you wish."

"No offense."

"I am not offended."

"Are you laughing at me?" she asked suspiciously.

"Oh, no, Rica, that would be very disrespectful."

"Ha ha ha. Shut up and kiss me."

He obliged, which she found delightful. The water was like cool silk against her and he was like hot silk, and everything was fine. She touched him again and again, half wondering if he would disappear in the same flash of light that had brought him.

His hands were all over her, his mouth was all over her, and soon enough she was climbing him like she used to climb the biggest tree in the orchard. He stopped her with his hands and easily lifted her out of the water, laying her on the bank.

"It is easier the first time to not be in water," he told her, and then dipped his head and sucked the moisture from her nipples.

"Whatever you say," she groaned. His head moved lower and lower, his tongue flickering out to caress her navel, her mons, her sweet inner folds. She had thought she was ready for him before, but the terrible need that swamped her was a new thing, a huge thing.

He carefully spread her wide for him and started to ease inside her, and she was clumsy in her eagerness—God, it felt like she had been waiting *forever*—but he stopped suddenly, just as it had started to become painful. He wriggled back down until he was licking and kissing her between her thighs again, until she was clawing at his back. Until that sweet dark heat she had previously only been able to bring to herself was coursing through her, spreading out from her stomach in dizzying, delicious warmth.

He entered her while she was still vibrating and this time there was no discomfort, only sweet friction—she'd never known friction could be so glorious. She had to give voice to it and her hoarse screams forced the birds to give wing, and it seemed for a moment she was spiraling up with them, flying with them, and she never, never wanted that moment to end.

Chapter 6

Sixty-eight sunrounds later ...

S"The rabbit," Rica announced, "is dead."

Shakar, who had just come in from watering the cattle, looked surprised. "What is a rabbit? Do you require a new one?"

"It's a smallish brown and white—never mind, look, I'm pregnant."

"You are ... with child?" A slow smile of delight was spreading over his face. "Truly?"

"Yeah."

"But how do you—I admit this is a very mysterious thing, a woman-thing."

"There's nothing mysterious about peeing on a stick—not that we do it that way anymore. I haven't had any flow since you came here, so I put a few things together and sent a blood sample to Central. You're—happy?" She realized she had been holding her breath, and let it out with such a woosh she was momentarily dizzy. "That's great." "Great" sounded inadequate, so she added, "Really really great. I wasn't sure what you would think. *I* don't know what to think."

"But that is wonderful!" He had started to sit down, but

then jumped up and prowled around the room. "Only think, a new prince or princess!"

"*Will* the baby be a prince or princess?" she asked quietly. "I thought you had turned away from all of that."

He stopped in mid-pace. "I did not turn away from being my father's son . . . only from being home."

"Uh-huh."

He came to her and put his big hand on her stomach. "How will you do it?"

"Do what?"

"Have the baby. You cannot do it here on the farm alone, with only me to help you. I am not knowledgeable in such things."

"No, I guess we'd have to go into town. We'd wait until it was close to my time and I guess we'd . . ." She trailed off, troubled. It was the exact problem that had been worrying her. "I could get Daran to watch the animals for me . . . heck, his family has been angling to get their hands on this place for a generation."

Shakar was silent. She bore the silence for a minute or two, then asked, "Why don't you say what's on your mind? You want to go back."

Still he said nothing.

"Come on, Shakar. You miss the SandLands."

"I think . . . I think it was you I wanted," he said, almost apologetically. "I thought, all this time, it was a place I wanted. But it was only you. I do not mean that I dislike your home."

She grinned at him. "I'm not offended, Shakar. That's probably the nicest thing anyone's ever said to me. But we have a little problem. And it's gonna be a big problem, soon enough. A blessing, as my mama would have said. But a complicated one. Got any ideas?"

He hesitated.

She said, "Better spit it out and get it over with."

"I do not wish you to birth the child here, alone save for me."

"Gotcha."

"I do not wish you to spend your last days of confinement in the town, away from both our homes."

"Uh-huh."

He paused again. "I would wish for Good King Sekal to see his son-by-his-son."

"So: The bottom line is you want to go home."

"Yes. I want to go home. But also, you should not give up your home to please me."

"Give up? Shakar, we can go back and forth whenever we want. Probably. Assuming the machine hasn't popped a screw loose or something."

"It seems . . . unnatural. To use a machine to go back and forth."

"I should have known you'd be a technophobe," she teased. "Look, I know you're used to magic portals just opening up out of nowhere, but I'm telling you, this way is better."

"It is not dangerous in any way?"

"Let's put it this way: My dad loaded that thing with so many fail-safes, if everything's not exactly right, we just won't go anywhere. We won't be like Jeff Goldblum in *The Fly*. Never mind. It's safe, Shakar. I'd never risk you or the baby if I wasn't totally sure."

"Hmmm . . ."

"Why not visit the home place, make nice with the future grandpa, all that good stuff? I can let Daran have a plot or two in exchange for watching the place while we're gone." *Why am I trying to talk him into this?* she asked herself. *Because I don't want to have the baby alone on a farm with just a prince to help me. That's why.*

"It seems," he said, giving her a warm look, "that you have thought of everything."

"I'm pretty bright like that," she replied, and leaned over to kiss him. His response was enthusiastic, to say the least, and after a moment she heard the plates crashing to the floor and felt herself bend over as they both hit the table.

"Good in theory," she groaned as his hands were busy opening her shirt, baring her for his mouth, his hands. "But hell on the back."

"As you wish," he said, and picked her up (it still amazed her that he could do that), and hurried down the hall into the small bedroom. They fell to the bed together, his mouth on her breasts, teasing her nipples, pulling on them with his lips.

"I really really *really* love it when you do that," she sighed, stroking his coarse hair.

"I really really really love to do it. You taste . . . wonderful. Wonderful, Rica."

Wonderful, Rica, she thought, helping him help her out of her clothes. She had lost count of the number of times he had said that in the past weeks. And she thought he was pretty wonderful, too. He was like a dream come true, falling out of the sky and into her life, her love, her prince.

She grasped his pulsing cock, gently squeezed, and his tongue swept past her teeth. They nibbled and kissed and she raised her knees for him, felt him slide inside her with a sweetness that left her amazed every time—it was as if they had been made for each other. Corny, but true.

"Oh, Rica . . ."

"I love you," she told him. And telling him was the same as it had been the first time: amazing, awe-inspiring.

"And I, you, my own."

She braced herself, then wriggled until she was on top of him, the way she liked, the way they both liked. Her breasts hung down for his mouth like exotic fruit, and he gobbled at them and sucked and licked, while she rode him to orgasm, until they were both spent.

"Okay," she said, straightening from her father's machine, the thing he had built to please her mother, and keep her mother. "Everything looks good. Stand over here. Pretend you're in one of those old episodes of *Star Trek*. Never mind," she added as he opened his mouth to ask the inevitable question. "Just stand there on the pads. I'll program it to toss us in thirty seconds."

"Toss?"

"It's just slang. Don't worry, you won't feel a thing. Probably." She fiddled with the controls, thinking that anyone but her father's daughter would have been lost. Her father had been almost ridiculously smart, and so he had built a machine that he understood. The fact that anyone who didn't hold a doctorate in spatial dynamics would be lost had likely never occurred to him.

But she had practically been weaned on this machine. Her earliest memory was of toddling out to the barn carrying tools for her father.

"It seems very strange to me," Shakar commented. "You are a credit to me."

"That didn't sound *too* smug. What do you mean, credit?" She went to stand beside him.

"You are beautiful *and* wise *and* self-sustaining *and* with child *and* kind *and* charming."

"I've got it all, baby," she joked, covering how embarrassed and thrilled she was, and the machine tossed them.

Chapter 7

"No, no, no, no, no, no, no, *no!*"

"Lois, dear, it's *my* wedding."

"Mom, this isn't a wedding, okay? The king waving his hand over you and pronouncing you 'mated' isn't a wedding."

"Well, hon, he's the one in charge. If we were in England and the queen pronounced you married, wouldn't you believe her?"

"Look, I didn't have a wedding, okay? And Anne didn't, but by God, you're gonna. You're *gonna.*"

Gladys gave her daughter a look. "The older you get, the more like your father you get."

Lois grinned. "No need to be nasty."

"So you're saying you'd like the white dress and an organ and finger food?"

"I'll settle for vows."

Gladys crossed her arms over her chest and, for a split second, looked exactly like Lois starting to get in a temper. "When you're my age, sunshine, you don't even need the damned vows."

"Don't be stubborn," Lois coaxed.

"Look who's talking!"

"Well, whose fault is that?"

"I think we just decided it was your father's fault. And where's Damon? He would probably take my side."

"That big chicken is trying to stay out of this. So's the king. I guess they're waiting to see what we decide."

"What I decide, dear."

"Aw, c'mon, Mom. Don't you want a proper wedding? You and Dad had a justice of the peace."

"Well, we had to," Gladys said reasonably. "You came along five months later."

"Not even any flowers!"

"They aggravate my hay fever. That's why I love this desert climate. So dry."

"So's an oven." Lois was mustering the perfect argument to bend her mother to her will when she heard the sound of galloping feet and suddenly Shakar burst into the sunroom, dragging a tall, big-boned, dark-skinned woman by one hand.

"Oh, hey," Lois said. "Welcome back. You're a little out of the loop, so let me bring you up to date. Anne and Maltese—"

"My woman is with child," Shakar burst out. "I fell into her world and swam in a pond and fed large animals."

"*Okayyyyyyy,*" Lois said. "I guess *I'm* out of the loop."

"Lois, where is the good king my father?"

"Oh, he's cowering in the halls somewhere. And don't think of him as the good king. Think of him as my new stepfather."

Sekal blinked at that, then said, "I wish to present Frederica Callenbra, of Callenbra Hold. Rica, this is my sister-by-mating, the good princess Lois, and her dam, soon-to-be-queen Gladys."

"Soon to be queen," Gladys mused, shaking Rica's large hand. "Queen. I hadn't . . . I've been so caught up in everything else . . . and Sekal asking me . . . I hadn't thought . . . hadn't realized . . ."

"Nice to meet you," Rica said. Lois was finding it hard to look away—Rica was easily the tallest woman she'd ever met, and with some real meat on her bones, not an emaciated supermodel type. Striking bone structure. And a manner that was almost . . . what? Dignified, she decided. "I've heard a lot about you."

"You're going to have a baby, then?" Gladys asked. "Congratulations!"

"Yes, we have much joy, we will find the king and there will be . . . Gladys, you should not be surprised. Did you not know? My father wanted you for his mate from the moment he gazed upon you."

"I did know," she replied steadily. "But I don't know anything about being queen. I'm just an office manager. I mean, I was back home."

"Better you than me," Lois said. "And if you can run an office full of accountants without committing double homicide, you can probably help Sekal run a kingdom."

"Sounds reasonable," Rica agreed.

"After a proper wedding ceremony," Lois added.

"Oh, hush up," she-who-would-soon-be-queen said.

"My king, may I present Frederica Callenbra, of Callenbra Hold. Rica, this is the good king, my sire."

"It's nice to meet you, sir."

The king looked confused. "I thought you were a-hunting," he said.

"Sir, I deeply regret any worry I caused you when I vanished ere these many—"

"But you have only been gone three sunrounds," the king replied.

"Day sunrounds or years sunrounds?" Lois muttered to

Damon. They had come to the throne room to be officially presented to Shakar's woman, and Maltese was standing on the king's other side. Anne was in another meeting with the lost ones, still hard at work deciphering the language. As her work was considered more important than mere socializing, however official, she had been left undisturbed. "I still don't get that."

"Days," Damon muttered back.

Meanwhile, Shakar was sputtering. "Three . . . no, sire, I have been gone almost an entire . . ." He trailed off. "I have been with Rica for some time. We only now came back. And—"

"I'm guessing time runs on a different track back home," Rica said. "It's been . . . what? A couple of days here? Not quite? But you were with me over two months. Long enough for us to . . . you know."

"I am certain I would have fretted, my son, if you had been gone longer," the king assured him.

"But as it is, we pretty much didn't notice," Lois added. "Sorry."

"Then if you had no worry, I did not miss—"

"Ah," the king said. "So you do remember."

"But, my king, I have found my mate."

"And I am sure she is very fine," the king said, giving Rica a warm smile, "but in fact, you—"

"It does not matter if I am here or not here," Shakar interrupted. "I have a mate."

"In fact, my son, you—"

"I will not allow this."

"Son—"

"I will not."

"Shakar."

"Father, that is my last word on it."

"*Prince Shakar.*"

Shakar's teeth came together with an audible click and Lois's eyes went wide. Gladys went to the king's side and whispered in his ear, and after a long moment Sekal nodded.

"She-who-will-be-my-mate wishes your m—wishes to hear Rica speak on this."

"Sir?" Rica said, looking startled.

"My son the good prince who has no manners is your mate?"

"Well . . . yes, sir. I mean . . ." She looked over at Shakar, whose golden skin was decidedly flushed. "Nothing official ever happened, but in the last couple of months it was just the two of us on my farm and we fell in love. I came with him today because he wanted to see you. All of you," she added, looking around the large room. "He missed all of you."

"The important thing to keep in mind," Lois joked, trying to lighten the tension, "is that we didn't miss him."

"The reason I ask, Rica, is because my son had responsibilities when he left. When he was gone for . . . a couple of months. And those responsibilities remain."

"He's already married, isn't he? It's something awful like that, or you two wouldn't be so upset."

"No, he is free to take a mate. And they are free to take him. You see, when the Bridefight was scheduled not long ago, we decided to also have a Groomfight. My youngest son the good prince was free at the time and seemed to welcome the idea. He has always . . ." The king shook his head. "What I am saying is this: In two sunrounds, females from all over the SandLands will come, and they will come for one reason—to battle for the hand of Shakar."

Chapter 8

"So!"

"Rica . . ."

"Were you saving it for a surprise?"

"It is not the way you—"

"Do *not* be telling me it's not what I think, buddy-boy. Not unless you want to have a black eye at your own Groomfight."

"There will be no Groomfight, because I have a mate. This is what I was trying to explain to my father. I will not participate. We will leave," he finished, looking almost as desolate as he sounded, "and it will not affect us."

"Not *affect* us? Are you blind, or just crazy? It's affecting us right now! And there will be no running away. You can get that straight right now." Rica whipped off her yellow work shirt—thank all the gods she had a small tee underneath—and flung it at the small stool in the corner. "We're going to stay here and take *your* medicine."

"Rica, you cannot fight pure—"

"Oh, here we get down to it. I can't fight a purebred. I know what a Bridefight is, my mama told me all about it, how sometimes the princes take mates that way. I never heard of a Groomfight, though."

"When he saw how happy Damon was with his mate," Shakar said dully, "my father and Lois—"

"Don't blame this on *me*," Lois protested. "All I said was maybe the girls could get a chance to fight for the guy they wanted. Next thing I know, you're all set up for *The Dating Game*, SandLands style. If you didn't want to do it, you had plenty of time to put a stop to it."

"I know," Shakar said miserably.

They were in yet another small room off the grand throne room, and Rica was glad. She would have felt weird chewing Shakar a new one in such a grand room. And in front of so many people. But this one was a little more to her taste, and she didn't mind that Damon and Lois had followed them. She kind of liked Lois.

She wasn't sure how she felt about the king. And Gladys, the older lady, had suddenly begged for his assistance in writing her vows, whatever that meant, and off they had gone. Which was probably good, since it gave her time to ream out her boyfriend

(husband?)

and recover from the surprises of the last ten minutes.

"Let's get back to this other thing. I can't fight purebreds? Pure SandLands girls, is that right?"

"No, you cannot." Shakar refused to be shamed, which was annoying. His voice was very firm as he continued. "I believe we have already established that you are a fine female in every way, but there are some things even you cannot do. And the baby must be safe. At all times, the baby must be safe."

"Too bad we didn't hide out long enough, huh?" She knew she sounded cruel; she *felt* cruel and didn't care. "That's what it was all about, wasn't it? All that shit about finding yourself. You were hiding from the Groomfight. And once you figured it was long over, then all of a sudden you're hot to see home and Dad again."

"That is not—"

"Don't you get it, Shakar? It's not even that you didn't tell me about the Groomfight—that's bad enough—it's that you hid, you *hid away* from your job."

"I have no defense," he said after a long silence.

"Well," Lois began, then stopped. "That's really all I had. I, uh, I'm sure it's not as bad as it—uh—"

"I require your assistance, Lois," Damon said suddenly, startling them all. He'd been so quiet Rica had forgotten he was there. "In another room. Not in this room."

"Right. Well, I'm here to serve. We'll—we've got to go. I'm sure this will all—we've got to go."

"You might as well take him with you," Rica said. "I'm done with him for now."

"Rica . . ."

"As you wish, good lady," Damon said, and then he grabbed Shakar by the scruff of the neck, as if he were a big blond naughty puppy, and literally hauled him away.

Rica almost smiled.

"Damon, remove your hands from me at *oncmmmllpphh!*"

"Like that? Is that gonna work for you?" Lois asked him. Damon had slid him into the wall like a big tiddlywink . . . it was really sort of funny.

"I have sufficient troubles," Shakar retorted, standing and straightening his hair—which was a mess, to put it mildly—"without you being cross as well."

"That is unfortunate, my good brother, because you've earned this scolding—possibly a beating as well—and you will accept it as a man does, as opposed to cringing and hiding behind a woman."

"Dude: What were you *thinking?* Hey, it's great that you found a girl, she seems really—well, great. But cripes, what a mess you've landed her in!"

"She is in no mess, because there will be no fight."

"It sounds to me like there is. Rica doesn't seem to be the type to just take off. Of course, you've known her longer. About two months longer, is that right?"

"I wasn't hiding," Shakar said woodenly. "I really did leave to hunt. The rest was . . . wonderful chance. It is true, I stayed with Rica and missed the Groomfight—thought I missed the Groomfight—but it was because I was happy with her."

"Uh-huh." Lois was skeptical, but the guy looked like a whipped hound already, so she tried to ease up. "Your dad seems kind of mad."

"And if Rica does not fight, he will get much more mad," Damon said.

"Then he will get much more mad, because Rica *will not fight.*"

"Well, it's not to the death or anything, right?"

"The baby must not be harmed. And Rica was not birthed here. She is from your world," he said, nodding at Lois.

"Oh, I get it. She doesn't do the Puma thing. Yeah, it doesn't seem like it'd be a fair fight. But I think a pregnant woman knows what she can and can't—"

"It is worse than that," Damon said. "I begin to see Shakar's problem. It is not just that Rica could be harmed . . . she will not win. And the winner will be Shakar's mate. Not Rica."

"Right now, that suits me fine," Rica snapped, but Lois saw the almost imperceptible spasm of pain that crossed her face.

"What are you doing here? We left so you could have some privacy."

"Well, I couldn't hang around in there all day, could I?"

"Okay, okay, everybody just try to calm down. Stuff doesn't have to happen right this second, does it? Rica, let's find you a room. You can get yourself sorted out, maybe rest up, and then we can go kick Shakar's ass some more. Right? I mean, standing around like this . . . it's cathartic as all get-out, but we're not getting much *done*, see what I mean?"

"I'd love to see a bedroom," Rica said, sounding so surprised and grateful, Lois was embarrassed she hadn't thought of it sooner.

Chapter 9

". . . And . . . and that's just how I feel, Sekal."

"It will be as you wish, my Gladys."

"I'm sure it sounds very very dumb to you, but . . . did you just say it was okay?"

"Yes."

"Oh."

"You may have as many vows as you wish. I also will recite as many as you require. In fact, I must apologize: I did not consider your traditions when—"

"Never mind about that, Sekal. If where I came from was so great, I'd probably still be there, right? I'm just so surprised you—I mean, you don't have to do vows, I thought they were kind of silly myself, but Lois wouldn't let up, and—and—"

"It is little enough, and it pleases you." He smiled at her, his large lavender eyes—Damon's eyes—seeming to sparkle. She had never seen such eyes in her life, and had thought she would never be used to them. But she was. It was almost frightening how quickly she had gotten used to them. "I would do much to please you, Gladys."

Oh that is so much nicer than "Move over, Wide Load."

"Thank you, Sekal. I feel the exact same way."

"Do you think sufficient time has elapsed?"

"Beg pardon?"

"For the children to scatter and plot strategies. That *is* why you dragged me out of the throne room this morning, yes?"

Gladys could feel her face heat up, but managed to smile back. "Yes, I guess you caught me."

"Your concern for a prince who is not yet yours-by-mating greatly warms me, Gladys. You will make a fine queen and a fine dam to my children. Even if the prince is behaving like a dar—like someone who does not know how to behave in matters of honor."

"She's pregnant, Sekal," she said soberly. "And they're in love. It changes things. It changes . . . everything, I guess. Don't you remember what it was like?"

Sekal shook his head. "I am an old man."

"That's not true at all."

"Only a future mate could say such a thing and not be telling a false tale," he teased.

She ignored that. "Besides, you just said—you said you'd do a lot to make me happy. Well, where in the world do you think Shakar gets it from? Not only is he trying to keep Rica happy, he's got the baby to think about. He's willing to make you mad and risk—I don't know—exile? I guess some pretty terrible things happen if he doesn't let her fight."

"Yes," he agreed and looked, for a moment, like the old man he had claimed to be. She found it more shocking than the fact that she had to think up marriage vows to keep him distracted. Gladys never thought of herself as old, but she wasn't exactly a puppy anymore. And Sekal had grown children, too. Neither of them were kids, that was for darned sure. But somehow, to her he had always looked strong and beautiful and . . . and timeless. Kingly. "Some pretty terrible things."

"Well, maybe we can head back and talk about it. I'm sure we can all figure something out. I'm sure Shakar will remember his manners and I'm sure you'll watch your temper."

"Will I, my Gladys?"

"You'd better." But she smiled to take the sternness out of her words.

Rica had been in her mother's land about, she figured, six hours, counting travel time from the jump-off point. And one thing her mother had never mentioned was, the pillows weren't stuffed with feathers.

Rica didn't know *what* they were stuffed with, but they looked like shiny black beads . . . except they were soft. She'd been in the middle of a real circuit-clearing temper tantrum when she realized. What *was* that stuff, anyway?

She picked up a bead and examined it. Part of her knew exactly what she was doing: she had a big problem she didn't want to face, so her mind was casting around for things that she could face. Like pillows without feathers.

She squeezed a bead. It squished, but didn't make any noise or squirt—thank goodness. She'd been half afraid the thing had been stuffed with beetles . . . that's what they looked like, beetles without legs, except squishy. It was—

"Rica, dear? May we come in?"

It was that Gladys. The king's sweetie. And she said "we" so Rica figured the king was with her. Good. She tossed the bead over her shoulder, crossed to the doorway, and held the curtain back.

"Hello. Come on in. It's your room, anyway," she added dryly, and the king smiled at her. Why . . . he looked just like Shakar when he smiled, all open and boyish. He had a downright pleasant face, come to think of it. And those eyes were really something. Small wonder Gladys looked at him like she looked at a rock star. "I made all the servants go away, but I could get you—"

"You need not be in our service, Rica. We came to be sure your needs are being met. And I must beg your forgiveness for what happened earlier. It seems my son did not inherit his stubbornness, pride, temper, or poor reaction to surprise from his mother." Sekal quirked an eyebrow at Gladys. "Or so it has been shown to me."

"Sir, I appreciate you and your lady coming by to make nice, but if there's been a screwup here, we all know it's not *your* screwup." *And what's the deal with your pillows?* she wanted to add, but managed to stop herself in time.

"Ah . . . yes. About that. Rica, I would beg you to never think I wish any harm to befall you, but—"

"You don't have to explain, King Sekal. Your son made a promise and then tried to get out of it. I imagine it's doubly bad if you're a prince and you try to shirk duty."

"Yes," he said simply. "It is doubly bad."

"But see, the thing is—I'm glad you came by, because I want to make sure we're all clear—the thing is, when I get over being mad at the big cabbage-head, I'm going to want to be with him. After I beat him severely. Possibly more than once. So I better fight. What I mean to say is, I'm *going* to fight."

"Dear, are you sure—"

Sekal cut her off, and Rica could see how that surprised Gladys. The old guy must feel pretty strongly about what was coming. "Rica, this is how I know you are already my daughter-by-mating. You do not 'shirk.' I am filled with pride to hear you speak thusly. But I must not set aside my concern for the new princeling—"

"Or princessling," Gladys added.

"Yes. Do I understand correctly, your dam was from my land?"

"Yes, sir. She fell through a thin spot and mated with my dad, and they had me."

"Then perhaps you know a bit of what would be required of you at a Groomfight. It is not to the death, of course, but you would have to physically triumph over those whose dams *and* sires came from here, and that I fear—"

"Sekal," she interrupted—and now *he* looked surprised. She figured not a lot of people cut off the king. "Can I tell you something? You and Gladys? Something secret?"

Chapter 10

Shakar took a deep breath and paused outside the room where his family was breaking the fast. He had—how did Lois put it? "Screwed the pooch," that was it, that was the term for an error—several errors—of abysmal judgment. His father thought he was a coward, and worse, Rica thought he was a coward. Worse even than that, his baby was in danger.

He had not honestly gone to Rica's world—not that he had had much say in where he went, or ended up—to avoid the Groomfight, but once there, he could not leave the woman he had searched for his entire life. He should have explained to Rica that they missed—he thought they missed—the event, which would have been personally embarrassing for his father, among other things.

His surprise to find he was mistaken was matched only by his horror when he realized that, in due accordance with tradition, Rica would have to fight.

Well. She would not fight, and that was how it must be. If it meant banishment, exile from the hot sands and cool purple sky he loved, then so be it.

He flung the curtain aside and strode in manfully, ready

to repair the damage he had wrought through carelessness. Rica should not pay the price for his mistakes; he would see to that, at least.

"—and then splat! Out of the sky he comes. Almost on top of me, thanks very much."

"Truly?" The king, Shakar was amazed to see, was hanging on Rica's every word, as were Damon, Maltese, Maltese's woman, Lois, and Gladys.

"Yeah, but he can haul a *lot* of wood, so he sort of re-deemed himself. You know, until lately," she added in a mutter.

"You've got to have another one of these jobbies," Lois said, passing Rica a plate overloaded with ghannas. "They're like a cross between a pear and a strawberry, except five times as sweet. And juicy! They gave you a bunch of nap-kins, right?"

"Lois, I'm stuffed. I'm gonna pop like a squished grape if you keep feeding me."

"Well, you gotta feed the baby. And one thing about this place—they don't have sunscreen but the food rocks."

Anne swallowed then cleared her throat. "When are you due, Rica?"

"I've got a long ways to go, Loo. I—"

"I'm sorry to interrupt, but my name is Anne, despite what you've heard. Loo is—" She cut her gaze to the left, where Maltese was grinning at his plate and finishing the last of his meal. "—a private nickname. But you were say-ing about your due date . . ."

"As best as I can figure—"

"I have come," Shakar declared, "to make amends with all."

They looked at him, Maltese still chewing. Shakar knew from a lifetime of experience that only the threat of war would keep Maltese from breaking his fast in the morning and possibly not even that—hadn't Lois said something about a fight with the dark travelers?

"Oh," Rica said after a silence that seemed, to him, to take a very long time to be broken. "It's you."

"Yes, it is I. I must—"

"You must sit down and eat, dear," his future mother-by-mating said gently. "Have you eaten a thing since you got back? You must be starving."

He glanced at Gladys, possibly the only member of the family who did not wish him dead, and found a smile. "As a matter of fact, I am most hungry. But that is not why I—"

"Then sit down, dumb-ass," Lois told him. "Before Rica eats it all."

"Oh, I like *that*. Here you've been jamming all this food down my throat like someone was paying you by the hour—"

"Ah, the good old days. Minimum wage, no benefits."

He sat. "I do not think you are understanding my purpose here this morning. I—"

"Was a total big loser," Lois said, "and you shouldn't forgive me, but if you *do* forgive me, I'll make it up to you with gobs of oral sex."

Gladys and Anne blushed to their hairlines; Rica laughed out loud. It was a fine sound and almost distracted him.

"I—"

"—have my father's temper and, occasionally, his poor manners, but I am not a bad man."

"Father—my king—"

"In case you haven't figured it out—my God, boy, you're slow—"

"No," Gladys said. "Just stubborn." Somehow, when she

said it, it did not seem like a matter to take offense over. In fact, it seemed as if all of them had decided not to take offense, which was beyond belief, because—

"Look, you screwed up, and I'm not saying I got over my mad-on, because I'm still pretty pissed. But we've all got jobs to do, and we'll do them, and we'll go on from there."

"Jobs to do?" Rica was right; he *was* slow. His father must have gone to her and tried to explain his position, and she of course explained that she would— "No, Rica! No! You must not fight! You—"

"Shakar—"

"*No!* I forbid it! We will leave *at once*. We will not return whilst this hangs over our heads. We—"

"—will be exiled?" Rica asked quietly. She had folded her fingers together to make a tent and now rested her chin on the top of the tent. She did not smell angry, only tired. "You'll lose everything, Shakar. Everything."

"Not everything," he replied.

"My son, sit down." His father had come to him, had hurried to his side, and Shakar was surprised to find himself on his feet; he must have leapt up when he shouted. He allowed his father to press him into a seat and accepted his pattings. "I was foolish not to see this for what it was last sunround. I assumed the worst and did you a sorry turn. But now listen: Rica has a stronger grasp, in this, than you do. She must do this for you, for the baby, and for herself. By doing this, she wins her mate rightfully, and secures a home for her infant. And word is spreading. *Think*, my good son. Everyone is talking about the strong dark mate you returned with; your care for her wellness is obvious. Who will risk the wrath of a prince? I am certain they will 'put on a show,' as my Gladys says, and then it will be over."

"But I can't—she can't—Sire, I cannot allow this thing."

Rica looked at him from the other end of the long table. She popped a kumquoss in her mouth and said, "Honey, what makes you think any of this is up to you?"

Chapter 11

"Maybe this is a silly question," Gladys began.

"O my Gladys, I doubt that."

"Wait 'til you hear the question," Lois suggested.

"But why can't we just cancel the Groomfight?"

"Cancel?"

"You know . . . send everyone home? Tell them the prince got married while he was—uh—abroad, and there's no point to it, and thanks for coming, and then they can go."

"I was wondering the same thing," Anne commented. "But I imagine there is a deeply ingrained cultural—"

"Cancel means to say you will be a host and then *not* be a host?" Sekal looked as horrified as Rica had ever seen him, and since the king had been having a rough week, that was pretty bad. "To invite people—females—from across the land, and then when they arrive after a long journey, say there will be no fight, that they came for nothing, and they must go home without even the honor of open combat?"

"Okay, okay, calm down, Sekal." Lois flapped her hands at him. "Your pills? See, I knew it wasn't going to be that easy. *Nothing in my new life is easy.*"

"I'm sorry we're such a burden," Anne said.

"I never thought about how difficult all this must be for you," Rica added.

"Aw, bite me, both of you. You're the sisters-in-law from hell, I swear. Nope, the only thing for it is for Rica to go down there and kick some major ass. *All* the ass, in fact." Lois looked a little anxious. "You've got a plan, right, Rica? Or at least a gun? Right? You're not just going down there for the sake of pride to get your ass kicked? There's a plan?"

"It will be fine," Rica assured her, which was a bit of a lie—she had no idea if it would be fine or not. But she would try. She would be her father's daughter and give it everything she had.

And she would be her mother's daughter as well.

"Where's Shakar? I mean, I know he's not exactly thrilled about this—"

"Oh, he'll be along," Lois said cheerfully. "He's tied up right now."

Rica frowned. "You mean in a meeting? A prince thing? Well, if it keeps his mind off—"

"No, I mean tied up. With rope. Except these guys don't use rope, it's like some kind of living—never mind."

"Maybe you'd better start over."

"Okay. Damon and Maltese were up at first light and set a trap, literally set a trap, and I guess he's been trying to get out of it so he can stop you from taking his medicine. Or something like that." Lois cocked her head, listening. "Oh, okay. He's almost out. They're all in their puma forms—you've seen Shakar's big cat, right? Right. Well, your mom could probably do it, too."

"If your mother could do it," Anne began, "isn't it possible that—"

"Hello, talking here!"

"There are times when I loathe you," Anne told her, "so much."

"*Anyway,* your disgraced sweetie will be here any second. Just in time to introduce himself to the crowd." Lois moved to the window and peeked out. "How many women would you say are down there, anyway? Boy, just think, all of 'em want to have hot monkey love with Shakar."

"How could they want him?" Anne exclaimed, also taking a peek. "They don't even know him."

"Oh, honey, you've never seen a picture of Prince William, have you? Never mind. Rica knows what I'm talking about."

"Who?" Rica asked.

"You know. Pr—"

"Rica." The king stepped into the room. "It is time. Are you ready?"

"Sure. Let's get it over with." She tried to smile and, after a moment, succeeded. "Once I get down there and in the middle of it, I won't be nervous anymore."

"That is how it is," the king assured her. "If you cannot flee, you must fight, and if you must fight, your dread departs."

"Someone should cross-stitch that on a pillow," Lois said.

"I'll get right on that," she replied, and allowed him to lead her to the lower level.

To the Groomfight.

Chapter 12

"It is an honor for me to see how many of you wish to participate," the king was saying . . . Lois couldn't *believe* how much Sekal was droning. *Get* on *with it, Chrissake.* Rica was probably a nervous wreck, ready to spew even if she didn't have morning sickness. "It is an honor," King Droney McDrone continued, "in light of this, our newest celebration, the Groomfight."

"I hope nobody on this balcony is thinking this is my fault," Lois said sharply.

"Oh no, why would we think that? It's not like you planted the idea in his head after the thing with Damon. Don't let your elastic conscience give you a moment of trouble," her mom said, in that deadly sweet/sarcastic tone Lois knew so well.

"—our son, the good Prince Shakar!"

Cheers. Waves. Feminine shrieks. It was like a Beatles reunion down there.

"I protest this and insist that all you good ladies immediately—*whggglllffff!*"

"Whoops, he's down again." Lois observed Damon and Maltese tackle their youngest brother, bearing him momentarily out of sight. She had a glimpse of Shakar's foot flying up and then disappearing as he was borne off of his chair. "Poor guy. He really needs to just accept what's going on."

"Yes, dear, you're the exact right person to give that particular piece of advice for this particular occasion."

"*Mooooommmmmm . . .*" *It's just as unacceptable to throttle your mom here as it is back home. It's just as unacceptable to throttle your mom here as it is back home. It's just*— "Whoops, here we go." Looked like things were (finally) starting up down below.

There was already a line forming on the opposite end of the arena; man, those chickies were itching to take a crack at Rica. There was an awful lot of whispering and meaningful looks, too. Lois wondered if the gossip—that Shakar was already married, so take it easy on the little woman—might backfire: *There's the ho that stole our man.*

She heard a crash from Shakar's general direction—nuts, she'd thought all the breakables had been removed from the general area. She didn't bother to look; she kept her eyes on the arena floor, where—there! The first challenger had transformed into . . . it looked like a small leopard, all spotty and sleek and, frankly, more than a match for Rica with her two legs and bare, vulnerable skin.

"Barbaric," was Anne's comment. "And not just the fighting. She doesn't seem to mind being unclothed in front of all these people. I guess that's something. I know I couldn't do it."

"Being naked is the least of her problems," Lois said, eyeing the competition.

"I agree. At least give her a weapon. Possibly six."

"Seems like there's a plan, though," Lois said. "Sekal's a little too relaxed, get me?"

"Mmmm."

Sekal was saying something—probably "Please don't kill my daughter-in-law"—but she lost it in the roar of the crowd. The little leopard started circling Rica, almost lazily.

And then . . .

"What on God's *earth?*" Anne gasped, but of course, they weren't on God's earth, this was another place entirely, and Rica . . .

Rica was a panther. A large, muscular, sleek panther of deepest black, a panther who left prints in the sand that were far, far bigger than Lois's hand, a panther whose muscles moved like velvet beneath the fur. Lois caught movement out of the corner of her eye and saw Damon, Maltese, and Shakar, all with their arms wrapped around each other (*awwwww*), all gaping at the enormous jungle animal Rica had become. She was . . . she was so . . . she was . . .

"My God, she's gi-normous! Well, sure—shit, Rica's a big girl, too, it makes sense—thanks for telling us so we *wouldn't worry or anything!*" Lois bawled down to the arena. "I mean, it might be considered, I dunno, *important information to share*, but shit, what do I know?"

"I'd say we have just deduced the plan," Anne said.

"Oh, please, look at that girl. She could *eat* all of them and still have room for lunch. This fight's over."

In fact, it did seem like Rica's transformation to her other form—her mother's gift, as it were—had made a powerful impression on the other participants. The small leopard had gone from lazy circles to wary backpedaling.

Rica popped back to her two-legged form. "Oh, come on," she said, and laughed a little. "There's gotta be *one* of you who doesn't mind having a spat."

"It's not just the color—though it's striking, and I've never seen anybody else here with fur like that. It's her size . . . she must be a head taller, at least, than all these other women. So, correspondingly, her animal form— puma? Panther? Well, it seems that—"

"Yeah, yeah, it's all a rich mystery just waiting for you to figure out. *Oooh*, there goes Shakar—he either knocked our husbands out or they let him go. Wouldn't you love to be a fly on the wall down there right now?"

"Now, I know you're mad—*oof!*" She fought for breath as he hugged her hard enough to make her gasp. "Okay, okay. Yes, I'm fine. And I know I should have told you. But to be fair, there were quite a few things you left out of our engrossing dialogue. So I figure, this squares us up. Now, it's not that I'm embarrassed or ashamed or anything, but only my mom and I could do that, and it kind of freaked Dad out, so I sort of got used to it being a private thing, and after they died, it was a *really* private thing, and there never seemed a good time to bring it up, and then with the baby and all—"

"Oh, Rica," Shakar said into her hair, squeezing her like she was—well, like she was a black shiny thing that should have been a feather but wasn't. "I'm *so glad* you're safe. Both of you."

"Yeah, well, Lois is right, you're a dumb-ass," she laughed, squeezing back. "I think part of the reason I didn't tell you is because I was waiting for you to figure it out. Didn't you tell me your mother was from my world? *You're* all half-breeds, too."

"Yes, but my good father is the king. Kings are different. They can do many things ordinary men can't." Shakar said it with total confidence, and Rica decided to save that one for another day.

Chapter 13

". . . And to treat her honorably and gently through all my sunrounds. This I so vow," the king added. "It is my vow."

Dead silence. Then Gladys said, "I don't know why I keep expecting a minister to appear out of nowhere and run this thing . . . now please say, man and wife."

"Man and wife," the king repeated obediently.

"Okay, now we're married."

"There, was that so friggin' hard?" Lois asked. "*Thank* you."

"Two weddings!" Gladys cried, and gave the king a loud smack right on the mouth. He looked surprised, but happy. "One right after the other . . . though I s'pose they were already married. Er, were they?"

"No one can say we're not married now," Rica said, reaching up and squeezing Shakar's hand, which had been hovering protectively over her shoulder since she'd left the arena. "Wasn't that part of the point?"

"It was a splendid surprise," the king said.

"Oh, yes," the queen added. "I thought it was impressive when you did that in your room when it was just the three of us, but to see it out on the floor like that in front of all those other girls . . ."

"Who got even paler." Rica smirked. "If that's possible."

"Attempt to be less smug in victory," Anne advised.

"You showed the king and queen?" Shakar asked, sounding wounded.

"Well, if you'd been there, I would have shown you, too. But you stayed away. All night long."

"I thought . . . I had brought disgrace upon us. I felt you would not welcome me to your bed."

"Well, see what happens when you stay out of the bedroom. You miss all kinds of things."

"There wasn't much of a fight, though," Lois said. "So, canceling it would have been a huge breach of honor, but all of them chickening out and not fighting wasn't?"

"There were a couple of dustups," Rica said. "Couple of them wanted to try their chops. It was fine. Nobody got hurt. Well, *I* didn't get hurt."

"And—I'm not *quite* done bitching and moaning yet, Rica, sorry—and the dark travelers, the devils, the horrible evil awful things, they turned out to be grumpy brunettes with speech impediments. Meanwhile, Rica's black—I'm not the only one who noticed, right? And her cat form is black—naturally. And everyone's all, *ooooooh*, that's so different it's cool. I mean, what is *with* you people?"

"I think any culture seems different and strange when you look at it from the outside. We would have difficulty explaining our society to our husbands, don't you think?"

"Well, at least Rica's from the same place as Mom and me. But how can you not know who Prince William is?" she joked.

"I've heard of *King* William, of course."

"Sure, sure, K—one more time?"

"Well, you know. The British royal family kept their titles but lost their money years and years ago, but in the history books, King William did a lot for England after his grand-mother—"

"Whoa. Whoa. Whoa." Lois turned to Shakar. "I thought you said you went to my world. Her farm in my world."

"I did. What is wrong?"

Lois turned back to Rica. "Your farm on Earth."

Rica laughed. "Of course not on Earth. Nobody can afford to live on Earth anymore."

"Uh-huh. This farm—barn animals, right?"

"Sure. You know, like krakens and bo'swill and, I dunno, some shrepen . . . animals you'd find on any farm, I guess."

"On any farm in the Twilight Zone! But . . . you can't be an alien, your slang . . . contractions . . . Anne says most languages don't evolve anywhere near the same way, so the chances that you'd be an alien who could speak perfectly accented English and who—"

"I was born on the farm," Rica said, mystified—why did Lois look so oddly at her? "Of course, I'm not from Earth, but my grandparents were. They helped build the ships . . . that's why we call ourselves colonists. We explored and made new homes for ourselves."

"So that place is not where my mother was from?" Shakar, thank goodness, was taking this a lot better than Lois was. It had never occurred to Rica . . . she assumed he . . . well, frankly, she did a stupid thing and assumed he knew things he couldn't possibly know. So who was the dumb-ass now? "Well, it is a very nice farm and I wish to go back."

"And now we can. We can go back and forth, like we planned."

"Wait a minute here, let's try to stay on track. So . . . Anne's from the past . . . the forties. And Mom and I are from the present. But you . . . you're from the future." Lois was walking around her admiringly. "No wonder you're so tall! Ah, but ultimately cool, as anyone whose parents were from Earth must be." She stopped prowling around Rica, which was something of a relief. "That makes you think, though, doesn't it? You guys all found the perfect wife . . . mate . . . and we're all from different times and one of us is from a totally different planet. I mean, what are the chances?"

"Well, my father built this machine that can move between worlds—"

"Of course he did, of *course* he did, he's some kind of supergenius from the future!"

"Um," Rica began.

"He probably built invisibility rays and flying cars, too. Did he have a gi-normous head?"

"Not that I ever noticed. So, Shakar, in all the excitement I never got a tour of this place." She seized his elbow and started to propel him out of the room.

"I guess the party's over," Anne said, sounding amused.

"I bet he *did* have a gi-normous head. How can I get her to tell me?"

"All this excitement. My! It's much more interesting here than in Cottage Grove."

"Do not fear, Gladys. It is quiet here," the king—her new husband—assured her. "For many sunrounds, nothing happens."

"Oh. Well, that's good. At my age I like a little peace and quiet." They were in the king's sumptuous quarters, standing beside the window and looking out into the darkening SandLands. Her home now. Odd how a girl born and bred in Minnesota could find comfort in the heat of a strange desert, under an odd sun.

"Your age, my Gladys? You are not so old."

"After the last couple of months, I feel old," she admitted.

"I like your smile marks," Sekar said, putting a big hand on her face and then tracing her laugh lines. "I like that you have seen many things. You will tell me many things?"

"I'll tell you whatever you want."

"Will you tell me that you cherish me?"

"I don't think we should base this marriage on lies," she teased, but when he didn't smile back, she said, "I do cherish you. I think you're wonderful. I—I didn't like my last husband. I like you a lot."

"Your first mate, with all respect, sounds like a fool."

"He wasn't the sharpest knife in the drawer," she admitted, "but back then, beggars couldn't be choosers. I was in trouble and he—"

"I do not wish to spend our first night as mates speaking of old mates."

"Me either." In a sudden fit of daring, she leaned forward and kissed him, half-waiting to be

("Susan Sarandon is older than you and her ass is in a helluva lot better shape.")

rebuffed. To her delight, not only did he kiss her back, but his strong arms came up and around her, cradling her. Making her feel safe. Cherished.

"Oh, Sekal," she whispered, staring into his wise purple eyes. "You're wonderful."

"I am only as you see me, my queen." He kissed her again, more urgently, and she tugged on his robes as they fell on the bed together.

"Forget it, Damon."

"But, my Lois—"

"No. I can't do it when I know my mom is somewhere else in the palace doing it."

"But it is one of the queen's duties to mate with—"

"Stop, *stop!*"

"But—"

"No way, Damon. Any other night but tonight."

"Oh, Lois."

"Sorry, pal."

He sighed. "Will morning never come?"

She laughed. "Cry me a river, Damon."

Rica stretched. "It serves me right, assuming you knew where you were."

"It serves me right, then, also. But it does not matter, Rica, truly. I thought I sought my mother's world, but as I have said, it was you I truly sought."

"Aw." She tightened her grip on his hand. "You keep talking like that, you'll make me forget I'm still pissed at you."

"And I at you, Rica. It was still a foolish risk."

"Are you kidding? Did you see all those scrawny little white girls? And their scrawny little kitty shapes? My grandma could have taken 'em."

"Perhaps that is so but I found the morning quite . . . aggravating."

"Race you back to the farm."

"Well, no, Rica, but soon? I confess," he added, pulling her to him, "I miss our privacy. It was our place."

"This can be, too. My folks could only have one world, and it sounds like your mama couldn't run off and leave this place without a queen. But we're luckier: we've got both worlds. Your home, full of family and fun and the people you love, and my home, with the animals and the work and the space. All that space . . ." She sighed, thinking of her home. Their home. Someday to be her baby's home . . . that, and the SandLands, where he or she would be a member of the royal family. But time enough to work all that out later.

"And the lake that was made by men," he added. "Do not forget that."

"Forget it? Honey, I've been trying to figure out how to bring it up. You know, it'd be really easy to design one. Then we just gotta get it built. Then—"

He stopped her with a kiss. "Then we will do many things and you will build many things to honor your father. But as for now . . ." He scooped her up easily enough, though he nearly whacked her head against the door frame. ". . . I never did see your room."

"It's the second star to the left," she sighed, enjoying the sensation of being carried. "And straight on 'til morning."

"What?"

"It's the doorway at the end of this hall." She wriggled free and he nearly dropped her. She looked up at him, laughing. "Race you."

Here's a sexy sneak peek
at Kathy Love's
FANGS FOR THE MEMORIES
available now from Brava . . .

Why would a gorgeous hunk like Rhys be fascinated with her? Sebastian had to be mistaken. But she had been in bed with Rhys. And he'd . . .

Her cheeks flamed, making her complexion a colorful pink, mottled against the purple under her eyes. She closed her eyes, releasing a hitched breath. She couldn't remember last night, but she could certainly remember the feeling of Rhys's hands on her when she woke up.

Heat drained from her flushed cheeks to pool in her belly, then lower. She'd never felt anything as wonderful as Rhys's fingers against her.

As if by their own will, her fingers moved to the buttons of her blouse. Not opening her eyes, she pretended it was Rhys's fingers loosening the buttons, parting the white cotton. The wisps of steam from the hot water filling the tub moistened her skin, and she pretended it was Rhys's kisses warming her flesh.

What was she doing? She'd never been the type to fantasize about men. And especially fantasies like this. But she'd also never had a man touch her like Rhys had. It had been so . . . thrilling.

She let her blouse fall to the floor, and she moved her fingers to the front clasp of her bra. The filmy material separated, and her nipples peaked against the humid air.

Embarrassed, but unable to stop herself, she brushed her fingers over them, trying to remember exactly how Rhys's lips had felt suckling her.

Her eyes snapped open at the sound of a quiet cough, and she spun toward the open doorway.

Rhys stood there, watching her.

She crossed her arms over her chest, trying to hide herself and to somehow hide what she'd been doing. But she could tell from the smoldering glow of his eyes, he'd seen.

The burn of embarrassment mingled with the fire those intense eyes created inside her. She so wanted this man.

His gaze left her covered chest, and he held her eyes with his.

She shifted slightly under the hunger she saw there.

"Sorry," he said, his voice was huskier than usual. "I thought I heard you calling me."

She stared at him. Well, her body had been calling him, but she didn't think her voice had. "I . . . No."

He nodded sharply. "Then I will leave you to your bath."

They stared at each other for a moment longer, then Rhys bowed slightly and left, pulling the door shut behind him.

Jane sagged against the sink, still clutching her breasts. This was impossible. It had taken every bit of her rational mind to not invite him to join her in the tub. What was wrong with her? She'd always been so practical, so reserved. Now she was acting like a wanton.

Rhy shut both Jane's bathroom and bedroom doors, and he still seemed to sense her desire pulling at him, begging him to come back to her. He stopped in the hallway, his own desire telling him to go back. She was his betrothed after all. They weren't married yet, but they would be soon, as soon as he could arrange it, and then that delectable body of hers would be his.

He nearly groaned, thinking about what she'd been doing when he'd arrived at her bathroom door. Her hands caressing her creamy skin, shaping themselves to the rounded curves of her breasts, her fingers teasing her swollen pink nipples.

He still remembered the taste of them. The heat of her body. His cock pulsed painfully in his trousers.

She was already his but—soon, he'd have her beside him every night.

Forcing himself to ignore his overly enthusiastic body, he searched for Sebastian. His brother had left him after their celebratory drink to talk with Jane again. Rhys was curious to see what Jane had told his brother.

Sebastian was in his room. He finished buttoning his shirt, then shrugged on a jacket.

"Where are you off to?"

"To the club." Sebastian combed his fingers through his blond hair. The locks fell into their usual, unruly tangle.

Rhys nodded. "I would join you, but I'm certain Jane already believes me a complete reprobate. I believe I should stay with her this evening and try to convince her otherwise."

Sebastian smiled, a puzzlingly amused twist of his lips. "Yes, I think you should."

Rhys frowned slightly, then went over to pick up a tie lying on Sebastian's bureau. How on earth would anyone get a proper cravat out of that skinny thing? He tossed it back onto the bureau.

"Where is Wilson?" Rhys had not seen their valet all

evening. Not that any of the brothers utilized the man much. They all agreed that if a man couldn't dress himself—well, he was truly inept.

Sebastian frowned, then his blue eyes widened. "Oh, Wilson. We gave him a holiday—for Christmas."

Christmas? That was right. Today was Christmas. Good Lord, Jane must think she was the one about to wed a savage. He hadn't even wished her a happy Christmas. And what of a proper Christmas meal—surely the staff hadn't forgone the meal because Elizabeth and Christian were away. And they had left on Christmas, too?

Rhys frowned. How very curious.

"I won't be at the club long," Sebastian said. "But I thought it would be nice for you and Jane to have a little time alone."

Rhys glanced at his brother, no longer bothered by his siblings being away. In fact, he quite liked the idea of having Jane to himself, too. He just wished he had thought to arrange a proper Christmas celebration, even if it was only for the two of them. He had so much to make amends for— he hoped she was an understanding woman.

"Have fun," Sebastian said. Again that knowing little grin was on his lips.

Rhys supposed his brother found him actually being taken with his betrothed quite humorous—especially after all the objections he'd had. Rhys had to admit it was mildly amusing. If he'd known what he was missing, he would have arranged for her to join him sooner.

The bath didn't have the desired effect Jane had hoped it would. She was too unnerved by all the events of the past two days to relax. Not that she wasn't tempted to hide in her room the rest of the night, but she was supposed to be watching Rhys.

She finished drying her hair, then brushed on a little mascara, hoping it would make her look a little less tired. Examining her reflection, she decided it didn't help much, but at least she was suitably clad, her turtleneck and jeans very modest.

She took a fortifying breath, then exited her room, going to find the "beautiful brothers."

She walked down the hall toward the living area. She pushed open one of the dining room doors, but no one was in there. She paused, her hand still on the door, and listened.

The whole apartment was silent as if not another living soul was there. Worry filled her. What if Rhys wasn't here? What if he left the apartment?

She softly closed the door and hurried farther down the hall. The hall opened out into a large living room. It was as lavish as the rest of the apartment, with more dark antique furniture covered in rich upholstery. But other than a cursory scan of the room, she didn't stop to study the decor too closely.

She rushed straight to another door at the far end of the living room. The door was ajar. She pushed the wood panel open and stepped inside.

Rhys stood in front of a huge stone fireplace, his profile to her, a drink held loosely in his hand.

She didn't say anything for a moment, too captivated by how gorgeous he was. The firelight glinted off his hair. The simplicity of the black sweater and black pants he wore seemed to enhance the width of his shoulders and the narrowness of his hips.

After a few moments, he glanced over at her. "Do come in. I promise I won't bite."

Karen Kelley knows just how
to heat things up in
TEMPERATURE RISING
coming in October from Brava . . .

A blue Oldsmobile pulled to the curb.

Oh crap! Troy had told her that his brother drove a blue car. She thought he'd said Lincoln, though. Whatever. She scrubbed her hands across her watery eyes, brushed her hair behind her ears, and pasted a smile on her face. At least she hadn't entirely blown the sale . . . yet. He turned the engine off, opened his door, and stepped out.

Tall and dark. He fit the description she'd been given. She smiled. Friendly, that's how she wanted to appear. Like they'd known each other for a while, rather than just meeting for the first time. Real Estate 101—Be their best friend.

"John?" She inwardly winced. She'd inhaled so many fumes that her voice was raspy. No time to worry about that now. *Shake it off. You're a professional.* She walked closer, smile widening.

The man hesitated before he walked around the front of his car toward the sidewalk where she stood. Jessica gave him a quick once over. Then went back for seconds. Troy certainly hadn't mentioned scrumptious, sexy and downright delicious. Not that he would think of his brother like that.

Her gaze blazed a trail past wide shoulders and across a

broad chest covered by a maroon Polo shirt before her glance slid downward.

Liquid heat coursed through her veins. There was just something about a man who wore his jeans low on his hips. It was almost as if he were telling the world he didn't really give a damn, and telling women he could fulfill their every desire.

His jeans pulled taut across nicely developed muscles as a booted foot stepped to the sidewalk. Drawing in a ragged breath, she forced her gaze back to his face and the knowing look in his eyes.

Oops. Caught staring.

She mentally shrugged. As sexy as he was, he should be used to appreciative looks from women.

"How much?" His roughly textured words scraped across her skin, leaving a heated flush in its wake.

Her thighs trembled. "You don't waste any time, do you?"

"We both know what I want."

"Wouldn't you like to see it first?" Did he turn a little red? She mentally shook her head. It was probably just the way the sun had hit his face.

He cleared his throat. "Why not get the trivial details out of the way, then we can . . . concentrate on other things."

His rich, southern drawl wrapped around her, causing a small earthquake inside her body. Three leisurely steps and he stood in front of her. Slowly, his gaze slid over her, lingering, touching, caressing.

At least six foot, four inches of raw male magnetism invaded her space. She inhaled and caught the scent of his musky aftershave. Much nicer than car fumes.

Pull yourself together. Business before pleasure. Yeah right, at this rate she'd give him the damned property and take the payment out in trade. *Okay, deep breath.* Jeez, what brand of aftershave was that? *Pheromones for Men?* She couldn't think with him this close. Turning away, she walked a short distance down the sidewalk to clear her muddled brain.

Think about the property.

The building was nice. Not too large. Taxes were low. Only single story, but it would make a great travel agency, which is what Troy said his brother wanted.

White, stone pillars gave the small commercial building a more prestigious appearance. She bit her bottom lip. Some of the ceiling tiles needed to be changed, water damage, but the owner had replaced the roof. A couple of the interior walls had rather large, gaping holes, though. In fact, the inside of the building needed a major overhaul. Personally, she thought the asking price a little steep, but the facts remained: it was in a prime location, the Texas town was growing, and this district had the fastest rate of improvement.

Only one teensy-tiny problem.

The eyesore across the street.

Triple X's flashed on the marquee of what used to be an old movie theater. If that wasn't bad enough, three scantily clad ladies had arrived a few minutes ago to stand on the corner. She grimaced. That wasn't good.

At least there were only three this evening. Two blondes, and she wasn't positive, but the third hooker's hair color looked deep purple. The one in question raised her hand and waved.

As unobtrusively as possible, Jessica motioned for them to leave. One cast her a grin and flashed a little leg. Great. She could see her sale gurgling as it choked its way down the drain.

Oh Lord, he was probably staring at them right now.

Maybe she could redirect his attention away from the "women of the night," and focus it on the property once again.

She wheeled around.

His gaze riveted on her chest.

Well, her boobs practically thrown in his face had certainly drawn his attention.

Her hand automatically fluttered toward the next button before she stopped the nervous habit from making her more exposed. She pointedly cleared her throat. He didn't get in any hurry to raise his head or appear a bit embarrassed at being caught staring.

"Two hundred," she stated, ignoring the little flare of desire that swept through her, and concentrated on the matter at hand. She wanted this sale. And actually, two hundred thousand wasn't a *bad* asking price for the land and building. She bit her bottom lip and waited for his reply.

Damn, he was cute. Why did he have to be such a distraction? Maybe they could get together after the deal was final. She inwardly smiled as naughty thoughts filled her head. She could easily picture them naked in bed, bodies pressed against each other. She sighed, wondering what he thought of her.

Conor Richmond thought the woman in front of him looked a little desperate. He wondered why she worked the streets. He figured her more for a high-priced call girl than a street hooker.

New in town, maybe? Like him?

Except she wanted to start a business. And the way she looked, it wouldn't take her long to have a whole string of *johns* begging for her favors and willing to shell out more than a couple of hundred dollars. If she cleaned up a little, that is, and bought some decent clothes. Her hose were ripped so badly she'd do better without them, and her skirt looked like she'd dug it out of the Salvation Army trash bin.

What had driven her to this way of life? Drugs? Her eyes were a little red-rimmed. She *could* be a user, although he didn't see any track marks running up her arms.

But underneath the smudge of dirt on her face and the worn clothes, he saw a sensuous woman, and he had a hell of a time keeping his gaze from straying. The amount of cleavage showing beckoned him to bury his face in her lush curves.

The view only got better. Her long, silky legs drew his attention even if her hose were shredded. They were the kind of legs made to wrap around a man. Pulling him deeper and deeper inside her hot body. Yeah, she was made for sex. The kind that got down and dirty.

A carload of boys driving by whistled and honked their horn. She looked momentarily distracted, then tossed a saucy grin in their direction as they laughed and sped down the street.

The smile transformed her face. Meant to pull an unsuspecting male into her web. He wasn't immune to her charms any more than the next poor sucker would be. But he wasn't her next customer, either. Sometimes he hated his job.

"Don't you think two hundred's a little steep?" he asked.

She wet her lips, her gaze returning to his. A temptress. Conor inwardly groaned.

"Not for what you'll get."

The way she said the words, kind of husky, made him wish just for a few hours he could pretend he wasn't a cop. Made him wish he hadn't seen her standing on the sidewalk. And made him wish that for a moment he hadn't thought she looked out of place and vulnerable.

Man, had he misjudged. She was a pro, all right. Her sultry eyes promised sinful delights. His gaze was drawn to her low-cut blouse when her hand moved toward the buttons . . . just as the gesture was meant to do.

His vision clouded as he remembered the way she'd walked down the sidewalk. Hell, how could he forget! Hips swaying seductively, and the way she'd slowly turned back around so he could see what he'd be giving up if she chose to keep going. He'd burned all the way down to his boots. No, she knew exactly what she did to him.

"And what will I get for my money?" he asked, wanting her to spell it out.

Her eyes widened innocently. "Why everything, of course."

Sliding his hand into his pocket, he emerged with a roll of crisp, green bills. Thumbing them, he drew two out and handed them to her. She took the money, looking a little confused, he thought, but decided it was part of her act. He pocketed the rest.

"A down payment?" she asked, staring at the bills.

Figured. She knew she had him by the balls. Why not twist a little harder? Get as much of his cash as she could.

"Is that okay?" He stepped forward. So near her scent washed over him, bathing him with erotic fantasies. She might look like she'd been sleeping in the streets, but she smelled oh-so-sweet. She raised her head. Her lips so close. So kissable. He ached to pull her into his arms and see if her mouth was as hot as it looked.

"I . . . suppose."

Too bad.

In one swift motion, he reached behind him, drew the handcuffs from the leather case hooked to his belt, and snapped them shut over her wrists.

A damn shame he couldn't have met her in another place. He had a gut feeling they would've been good together.

"Lady, you're under arrest for solicitation."

You gotta get it. That's
GET A CLUE
by Jill Shalvis,
available from Brava . . .

Cooper's deep blue eyes sparked, *flamed*, and the oddest thing happened to her. In spite of everything, a little ball of heat swirled low in her belly.

She had to be delirious. From the cold. From exhaustion. From her life sucking big-time. Awkwardly she hopped again, trying to pull her jeans back up, but they weren't going anywhere. Then she made one too many hops and caught her boot heel on the hem of the jeans. Waving her arms wildly, she struggled for balance.

Cooper merely stepped forward and caught her.

Fine. He could help her and she could die of mortification later.

But he didn't help. He put a hand to the middle of her chest and gave her a little push, making her fall gracelessly to the couch. Once again, the pink vibrator hit the floor and rolled to a stop at his feet.

They both stared at it for one beat before Breanne tried to bounce back up.

"*Stay*," he commanded.

Oh, no. *Hell, no.* She scissored her legs, meaning to kick him, either in the chin or the nads, she didn't care; she was going to take him down. *Now*.

But he just laughed low in his throat, and then again when she struggled to karate-chop him with her legs caught together by her own jeans. *Laughed*, as he crouched beside her, a big hand on either of her thighs and said, "Give in, Princess."

"I never give in."

Holding her down with ease, he reached for the fallen vibrator, lifting it up. The obnoxious thing still glowed neon-pink. "Never say never." Then he grinned at her in the firelight, looking just like the devil must look in the dead of winter with no one to torture. "This thing keeps showing up. Maybe you should claim it."

"It's *not* mine!"

"I don't know . . . earlier you were gripping it like it was your long-lost best friend." With a flick of his wrist, he turned it on.

The low hum filled the air, and with it came a buzzing in Breanne's ear—the sound of her brain coming to boiling point.

"Ready for use," Cooper said, suggestively waggling it in her face.

"Good." She struggled to get free, trying not to think about the picture she was presenting him with. "You can shove it up your—"

"Oh, no," he said. "Ladies first." He dropped the thing to the couch next to her, where it rumbled against the soft, buttery leather while he slid his hands down her legs to the jeans pooled between her knees.

"Don't even *think* about it," she choked out.

But he wasn't only thinking about it, he was doing it, fisting his fingers into the wet denim and yanking them past her knees to her ankles, where they caught on her boots.

His gaze met hers, intense and raw, and along with it a heart-stopping heat.

Did he have to pack such a sexual energy? She felt her entire body clench with a punch of shocking yearning.

"High-heeled boots," he murmured. "Ever so practical out here."

She stared down at the top of his head as he worked on stripping her. Her little triangle of white satin had not only slipped sideways, it was now riding up into parts unknown. She'd had a bikini wax two days ago—again for the rat bastard Dean—and judging from the very soft, very rough sound that escaped Cooper at her movements, he'd caught an eyeful up close and personal. "If I wasn't so tired," she murmured, sagging back, suddenly exhausted, "I'd kick your ass."

"Next time," he said, trying to untie her boots. The laces were iced. "I guess you were all prettied up for the honeymoon."

No. She'd prettied up for herself, to feel sexy, but she was not going to argue with a man when her pants were around her ankles; when she had a vibrator bouncing on the couch next to her, taunting her; when she had bigger worries, such as her panties, and what they still weren't covering. Shoving the sweatshirt down as far as she could, which was to the tops of her thighs, she leaned forward to hurry the process along.